# MISTWOOD

## LEAH CYPESS

GREENWILLOW BOOKS
*An Imprint of* HarperCollins*Publishers*

Mistwood

Copyright © 2010 by Leah Cypess

All rights reserved. No part of this book may be used or reproduced in any manner whatsoever without written permission except in the case of brief quotations embodied in critical articles and reviews. Printed in the United States of America. For information address HarperCollins Children's Books, a division of HarperCollins Publishers, 10 East 53rd Street, New York, NY 10022.

www.harperteen.com

The text of this book is set in 11-point Stempel Garamond.
Book design by Paul Zakris

Library of Congress Cataloging-in-Publication Data

Cypess, Leah.
Mistwood / by Leah Cypess.
p. cm.
"Greenwillow Books."
Summary: Brought back from the Mistwood to protect the royal family, a girl who has no memory of being a shape-shifter encounters political and magical intrigue as she struggles with her growing feelings for the prince.
ISBN 978-0-06-195699-7 (trade bdg.) — ISBN 978-0-06-195700-0 (lib. bdg.)
[1. Kings, queens, rulers, etc.—Fiction. 2. Magic—Fiction.
3. Loyalty—Fiction. 4. Fantasy.]
I. Title.
PZ7.C9972Mi 2010          [Fic]—dc22          2009023051

10 11 12 13 14 LP/RRDB 10 9 8 7 6 5 4 3 2
First Edition

 Greenwillow Books

To Tova,
  *my first reader*

Aaron,
  *my last (but not least!) reader*

and to Shoshana & Hadassah,
  *I hope you will read this someday,*
  *and know why Mommy was*
  *scribbling in those notebooks while*
  *she followed you around the playground*

# PART I

# SHIFTER

# Chapter One

She knew every inch of the forest, every narrow path that twisted and wound its way beneath the silver branches. They never should have found her. She should have been up and away long before the horses' scent came to her, and very long before the sound of men's whispering drifted to her ears. Through the trees or in them, even above them, she could have fled in an instant, or hidden herself so well that they could scour the forest for days and never find her.

Her ankle was hurt, or it never would have happened. So she told herself for days afterward. And even much later, when she knew much more, she still thought it might be true. Whatever instinct made her wait for the prince to find her, it was given strength by the effort it would have cost her to move.

Her forest was an old one, the earth covered with layers of moss and dead leaves, the huge trees covering the sky with vast foliage and wrapping thick roots around mounds of earth. It wasn't a wood that was easy to ride through—there were no straight lines or even meandering ones. No one would have dared blaze a trail here, and if they had they would have soon regretted it. And always there was the mist, rising through the ferns like tiny feathers, sometimes thinning to a layer of white on the ground and sometimes drifting in hazy clouds that tried to smother the trees.

Only a fool would ride here—a fool with an urgent need. And somewhere, in a stirring in the back of her mind that wasn't even a thought, she knew what they needed. She stayed where she was until the prince rode into the small clearing and reined in his nervous horse.

She knew he was a prince as soon as she saw him. Not because he was dressed like one; his black riding habit and green cape, while dramatic, could have belonged to any nobleman. His face was chiseled and sharp-jawed, but a bit too drawn to be regal. Nor was it his bearing. He was disheveled and tired, and right before he saw her he uttered a curse that would have fit the mouth of the coarsest peasant.

He reined in his horse, which *was* a beast fit for a king, and stared at her. "Will!"

The boy who rode behind resembled him closely enough to be his twin, except he was several years younger, barely in his teens. He gaped. "Is it her?"

"Who else could it be?" The prince leaned over his horse's neck, and—lowering his voice as if trying not to frighten her—said, "Isabel?"

Then she tried to run. She leaped to her feet and her ankle twisted beneath her, too weak to hold her weight. By the time she dragged herself off the ground, the prince was kneeling beside her.

"Are you all right, my lady?"

She struck at him, fingers curved into claws. The prince jumped back, but not fast enough. She left four diagonal slashes on his left cheek, and the bottom three had welled up with redness by the time he looked down at her. His eyes were so dark they appeared black, wide and wary beneath slashing eyebrows.

"Don't do that," he said, not even reaching up to touch his cheek. It was somewhere between a command and a plea.

Isabel snarled and lunged at him again, ignoring the pain that shot through her ankle. This time he jumped away fast enough.

"Rokan?" The younger boy's voice was high with fear. "What's wrong with her?"

"Hush, Will." His eyes still on hers, the prince stuck

his hand into his belt pouch and drew out a thin bracelet shaped of tiny metal links, with a crystal embedded in each one. Most of the crystals were pure white, but every third one was deep red.

"Isabel?" the prince said, very quietly, and extended the bracelet to her.

Her hand went up without her conscious control, as if from long habit it knew what to do. Not up to attack, but in a fluid, graceful motion, her palm down and her fingers limp. She did not move when the prince brought both his hands toward hers, though her arm tensed and trembled. He laid the bracelet on her wrist, and she let out a sigh when it touched her skin.

The prince fastened the clasp with one smooth movement. Then he took her hand, and she let him draw her to her feet, keeping her weight off the weak ankle. She felt dazed.

"Isabel," the prince said with a note of satisfaction in his voice. "By the Shifter's Seal on your wrist, do you swear to serve me and mine with all your abilities and powers, to defend us and protect us and keep us safe from all harm?"

She looked up at him and said, "What?"

He grinned then, his dark eyes gleaming, and she lost any hope of turning and running before it was too late. It was already too late. Something about that wide, unrestrained smile . . .

"I suppose we don't have to go through all that," he said. "The legends say we should, but—will you come to my castle with me?"

He waited for an answer, and after a long moment she nodded.

"Rokan," said Will, who was still mounted. "Aren't you forgetting something?"

"Oh, yes." The prince kept his eyes on her face, but there was an odd glint in them as he said, "I'm afraid you're going to have to wear clothes, my lady. They're very traditional where I come from."

She looked down at herself, then around at the dead leaves surrounding her feet. She spoke again. It had been so long that she was surprised at how easy it was, how readily her voice responded to her mind's command.

"Later."

The prince glanced at his younger brother, who was beet red, and then back at her. "Er—I think now would be better."

She shrugged, and when he drew a pile of fabric out of his saddlebag and handed it to her, memory began to return. "Turn around while I dress," she said.

The prince raised his eyebrows but obeyed. Will wheeled his horse around.

She put the clothes on—green riding pants and a white silk tunic—and felt comfortable in them as soon as they

settled on her. They fit perfectly. She tapped the prince on the shoulder.

"Better?" she asked, almost pertly. She had gotten dressed without even thinking about it, like it was something she had done a million times before. Maybe she had. She still didn't remember when, or why, but for the moment that didn't matter. The ease with which she remembered *how* was reassuring.

"Superb." The prince smiled at her, and she thought she should probably smile back but couldn't seem to figure out how.

He mounted smoothly and reached down to pull her up behind him. She wrapped her arms around his waist and laid her cheek against his back, and for a moment, an inexplicable moment, she wanted to cry.

The horse began to trot, and she closed her eyes. She didn't want to see her trees sliding past, sliding away. The prince's muscles were taut beneath the silk of his tunic. For the briefest of seconds, almost against her will, she shared the excitement she could feel running through him.

She schooled herself into unthinkingness, retreating deeper into her own mind until she couldn't feel the prince's body or the jolting of the horse, nothing but the wind against her face. Then she slid in deeper, until she couldn't even feel that.

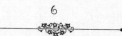

# PART II

# ROKAN

# Chapter Two

She woke in a satin-lined bed with green canopies hanging over her head. For a moment she had no idea where she was or why, and she kicked the sheets away in a panic. Her ankle twinged, and she remembered; but she didn't draw the sheets back up, and she didn't let go of the panic.

What had she been thinking?

Brushing away the bed's gauzy draperies, she put her feet on the floor and stood up gingerly, testing her ankle. Still sore, but she could walk on it. In two days it would be completely healed.

If the prince had come two days later, or two days earlier, she wouldn't be here now.

She took a few steps away from the bed and examined the room—my room, she thought with complete certainty.

A great tapestry hung across the wall to the left of the bed, woven forest scenes in muted green and white. The elaborate bed was all gold-trimmed green, as were the few low benches and chairs laid out along the sides of the room. Unbidden, a snatch of song leaped into her head: *For the Shifter's eyes are green, green, green, as green as the woods she loves. . . .*

Straight across from the foot of her bed were two vast windows with a long mirror between them. She limped over and looked in the mirror, with no clear idea of what she expected to see.

Her eyes were brown. So was her hair, which was filthy and hung in dark, limp tangles past her sharp chin. Her skin was pale, with regular but plain features—wide forehead, flat cheekbones, long thin nose. She was still wearing the clothes the prince had given her, and beneath them her body was lean and wiry. She stared at her reflection, certain that she had never seen it before.

"Isabel!"

She whirled away from the mirror, the name ringing in her head. *Isabel.* When the prince had called her by that name, it hadn't mattered; she hadn't possessed a name, couldn't remember ever having a name. But now, in these clothes, in this room, she knew she did. *Isabel.*

"Are you finally up?" the girl standing in her doorway

said with a small smile. "We thought you would sleep forever. You had Rokan quite concerned. He was afraid his trek into the Mistwood had been for nothing."

The girl kept smiling as she moved forward, the motion of her legs almost invisible beneath her long silk skirt. She was wearing a dark blue dress with a tight bodice and flared sleeves that would be impractical in a fight. Isabel watched her approach. There was nothing else she could do. In these clothes, in this room, as Isabel, she could not attack this girl simply for coming too close to her.

The girl halted when she was only a few feet from Isabel and scrutinized her. *She* had green eyes, and a wealth of curly blond hair that spilled around her wide face. "I'm Clarisse. Don't you remember me?"

Isabel shook her head.

"Oh." Clarisse pursed her full lips and tilted her head to one side. "Oh, well. No doubt you remember Rokan?"

"No," Isabel said.

"I see." Clarisse paused, looked her up and down, and smiled again. "Well, good-bye, Isabel. I'll leave you to get some more rest."

She turned and walked away without waiting for a response, and Isabel watched her go with narrowed eyes. She did not like that smile. It was too smug. Clarisse had come here for a specific purpose and had accomplished it.

She came, Isabel thought with a flash of clarity, to see me. To decide what she thought of me, and what she could get out of me.

It had been an attack, of sorts, and people did fight who lived in castles like these. Not with fists and feet and claws, but with words and whispers and influence. Isabel couldn't remember having been here before, but she knew. It was a fight, or rather a game, with many players and many rules and many strategies.

She smiled suddenly, feeling her blood pump through her veins. She didn't know how, and she didn't know why, but she was suddenly sure it was a game she knew how to play.

Two guards stood outside her door, brawny young men in blue uniforms with bright, shiny swords. When Isabel asked them where Prince Rokan was, they exchanged glances, looked at her, and then at each other again. Clearly, they had been told to guard her room but didn't know if they were protecting her or imprisoning her.

Reveling in her ability to discern that from an awkward moment, wondering where she had gained the experience to do so, Isabel tossed her head and said haughtily, "Well? Where can I find him? I must speak to him at once."

"Er—why don't you stay here, my lady?" one of the guards said. "We'll send for him."

"Nonsense," Isabel said. "I'll go to him myself."

The other guard straightened. "I'm afraid we can't allow you to do that."

She turned startled eyes on him, pretending this possibility had never occurred to her. "Can't *allow*?"

"We were ordered to guard you, my lady. For your own protection. I can't let you leave until the prince relieves me of my command."

Isabel eyed him for a moment, then stepped out into the hall.

He reached out. "Stop! I just said—"

Isabel looked over her shoulder, lifted her chin, and froze him with a glare. "You would dare lay a hand on me?"

His hand went still in midair, mere inches from her shoulder. Isabel turned her head and strode away, ignoring the twinge in her ankle.

Neither of them came after her.

The hall was lined with elaborate tapestries, depicting battlefields and romantic idylls in that awkward, stylized way that tapestries did, but the floor was uncovered and the stone was cold against her bare feet. She came to a stairway that curved down into a long pillared hall, and followed it without hesitation. She felt that there should be a long skirt sweeping behind her, and she almost turned to gather it up before she recalled that she was wearing riding pants. For an odd moment she was embarrassed by that.

At the bottom of the stairs was a deserted ballroom. She kept walking, knowing exactly where to go without any clear idea of where it was she was going. At the end of the ballroom, two thick wooden doors stood open, and a constant murmur of voices floated out through them.

Two guards stood at the entrance, right outside the room. They were much better dressed, and apparently better trained, than the guards watching her room. Neither so much as glanced at her as she stepped in front of the doorway, despite her bare feet and her clothes. Isabel hesitated, and her hands went to her hair.

It was a mass of tangled knots. She couldn't remember having ever brushed it. Isabel frowned. Why should she care about her hair?

She took a step forward so that she was out of the guards' line of vision. She raised both hands and brushed them lightly over her hair, then looked sharply at the guards to see if they had turned. They were still staring straight ahead.

She took one strand of hair and arranged it over her shoulder. It was long and silky, so blond it was almost gold. She brushed the strands carefully over the white silk of her tunic, then permitted herself a small smile as she strode through the door.

* * *

The Challenge Hour was almost over, and the court was restless and bored. Keeping his back straight so he wouldn't have to lean against the uncomfortable wooden throne, Rokan allowed his eyes to rove over the room. A large hall of maroon and gold, with glittering chandeliers and long mirrors, it seemed crowded and small with the mass of courtiers and ladies milling about on the carved wood floor. This was his thirtieth day of Challenge-sitting, and his last. After today, any challenge to his right to the throne of Samorna would be much more complicated than a straightforward declaration before the court.

Of course, many members of his court liked convoluted routes—in fact, thrived upon them. Rokan kept his eyes moving, noting the people who had been absent for the past twenty-nine days of Challenge-sitting but were here for the last. The soldiers, not one of whom thought he would be as strong as his father; the southern merchants, who feared he wouldn't be; the northern dukes, who had been waiting for decades for a weak king and were now hoping for him to be one. For him to fail.

I will not fail, Rokan thought, and scanned the room for his few allies. Such as they were.

His sister was there now—he hadn't seen her enter—leaning against the gold-patterned white wall, watching everything and everyone. Like everyone else, Clarisse was sure he was going to make mistakes, but she was waiting to step in and save him from himself. His younger brother was watching him with eyes alight, and Rokan smiled across the room at him. Willard, of all the people in the room, was the only one who had never even imagined that Rokan might fail. His blind faith made his advice fairly useless, but it was nice to have *someone* around who had confidence in him.

Albin, the high sorcerer, was currently glaring at him—or more specifically, at the scratches on his cheek. Rokan resisted the urge to touch them. He wondered if the Shifter had woken yet—or, as Will had speculated, if she ever would wake. Rokan hadn't noticed that she was asleep yesterday until the castle had come into sight. Its sprawling stone walls and clusters of soaring towers still impressed even him, and he had turned to see her reaction. But the wild creature holding on to him had been unconscious, her breathing so light that for a panicked moment he had thought she was dead.

She couldn't be dead. He needed her.

Rokan realized that his fists were clenched, and he hastily relaxed them, hoping none of the constantly watching eyes had noticed. The ride to find the Shifter would have been worth it even if they hadn't found her;

just to ride for an entire morning with no one but Will. It would probably be a year or more before he got to ride like that again.

"Your Highness!"

The shock of being addressed during a Challenge Hour drove all else from Rokan's mind, making his blood pound. He straightened almost eagerly, seeking the source of the threat.

Then the words sank in: *Your Highness*. This was not a challenge at all.

"Duke Owain," he said with some resignation.

The duke coughed loudly, his distinguished gray beard masking his expression. "I'm sorry, Your Highness, but I must ask your leave to depart. Lady Daria is feeling ill."

Despite himself, Rokan's eyes darted to the young woman beside the duke, who stood with her eyes lowered and a faint blush on her cheeks. He was willing to bet Daria was feeling fine. Owain had spoken for one reason: so Rokan would give the duke's niece a worried glance, and the court would note it.

Cursing himself for falling into the duke's trap, Rokan said, "Of course," and forced himself to meet Clarisse's eyes. Her face was studiously blank. This morning she had spent an hour warning him to control his impulses.

*Easy for her to say. I'm not made of stone.* But despite

his irritation, he knew Clarisse was right.

Rokan had imagined failing many times; imagined the consequences for himself and for all the people who now depended upon him. His father had spelled out his weakness many times: he cared too deeply, wanted too much, acted too quickly when his emotions were involved. And while Rokan had always secretly thought some of those were strengths, that didn't keep him from recognizing that they might be his downfall anyhow. His father had drilled into him the harsh reality that being a good man and being a good king were two separate, opposite things.

Though according to Clarisse, a stubborn refusal to accept harsh realities was another of his weaknesses.

Which brought his thoughts back to the Shifter, beautiful and feral and surrounded by mist. It was still difficult to believe that she had come with them, that she was here in this castle.

A murmur rose near the back of the room, surprised and slightly scandalized, and he knew the reason for it even before he saw her. For a moment he almost believed his thoughts had summoned her.

She was walking down the maroon carpet that led to the throne, apparently unaware of the way everyone was turning to stare at her. Her hair had changed, becoming long and blond, but everything else was the same. Her

wide eyes, her odd, proud beauty—and the way she was staring at him, directly at him, ignoring the crowd around her. The nobles were watching her, startled and speculative, and Rokan sat back.

It was still the Challenge Hour.

A thrill of anticipation went through him as the Shifter stopped before his throne. She was barefoot and dirty and in riding clothes, but something else about her was making the nearest courtiers edge away. It was possible that yesterday he had made the biggest mistake of his life. But the bracelet dangled delicately from her wrist. If he had done this right, she wouldn't hurt him.

If he had done this right.

The silence stretched unbearably. He tried to clear his throat and couldn't get his throat muscles to move.

Then she knelt gracefully on one knee but did not bow her head. Her eyes were on him as she spoke.

"Prince Rokan," she said. Her voice was clear and strong, something he hadn't noticed in the forest. "I come to serve Your Highness."

A surge of triumph rose and burst within him. As he straightened, a great bell rang in the distance and every person in the hall sank into a bow or curtsy. Every person but her. For a moment all Rokan could see were the backs of lowered heads and the startling dark eyes of the Shifter,

fierce and wild and trained on his face. She didn't have to bow; she was here to serve him, but she was not his subject, any more than a force of nature could be his subject. His heart beat faster, and he smiled at her exultantly.

The thirtieth day of Challenge was over, and he was king.

An intimate group gathered in the king's private audience chamber as soon as the Challenge Hour ended. It was clear to Isabel that Rokan would have preferred it to be even more intimate, but he wasn't given a choice. The moment he stepped off his throne and motioned for her to follow him, Will was by his side. Clarisse had been there even before that.

Isabel liked the audience chamber, and thought she had always liked it, though she had no specific memory of it until she stepped through the narrow doorway. The room managed to be cozy and stately at once, with two vast windows and olive curtains pulled back to let light flood in. The space between the windows was filled by an ivory couch that didn't quite fit the room but did appear to be the only comfortable seat in it. Clarisse went straight for the couch. Isabel, who had been headed there, too—*where I always sit*, a small, angry voice inside her whispered—stopped and focused instead on the painting above the fireplace at the far end of the room. It was a portrait of a man wearing an ermine cap, with small, narrow eyes below thinly arched brows, a long, large nose, and a short black beard. Though he had been painted in half-profile, something about the man's gaze was unnervingly direct; he seemed to be weighing the painter's worth and finding it wanting. It stirred a sharp memory in her, though she didn't know who the man was.

Clarisse flung herself onto the couch, reclining on her side as if posing for a painting, her head propped up by a small hand buried in her mass of hair. Almost reluctantly, Isabel tore her eyes away from the portrait.

"Well, well," Clarisse drawled. "That was very impolitic of you. You gave Rokan a real scare."

"She did not!" Will snapped. "She wears the bracelet, the Shifter's Seal. He had nothing to be afraid of."

Clarisse raised her eyebrows. "When reason starts having anything to do with what Rokan feels, let me know."

"Just because you don't agree with his reasons—"

"Be quiet, Clarisse," Rokan said tiredly. Instead of sitting, he leaned against the wall near the door, his head coming to rest against an elongated yellow tapestry. He was clean-shaven, but the resemblance to the man in the painting was unmistakable.

Four faint scratches marked his left cheek. Isabel felt

a hot rush of shame. The instinct that had guided her to declare her allegiance in the throne room drained suddenly away, and with a spurt of panic she wondered what she was doing here. She didn't belong. She didn't know how to act, or even where to sit. And worst of all, she had hurt him.

"I wasn't talking," Clarisse pointed out. "Will was."

"But you were about to interrupt him. I'm tired of arguing all my decisions with you. I decided to seek out the Shifter, and I did."

Isabel tensed, feeling vulnerable and exposed in the center of the room. There were cushioned wooden benches at both ends of the room, but she found herself reluctant to move that far from Rokan.

"Of course, Your Most Royal Highness," Clarisse murmured. "And how has she helped you so far?"

"That," Rokan snapped, "is what I'm going to discuss. With Isabel."

Clarisse shrugged. She clearly had no intention of moving.

Everyone looked at Isabel.

Isabel held her head up, swamped by a swirl of confusing, conflicting feelings. Chief among them was a fierce urge to protect her prince, but from whom?

*Her prince* ... The possessive came to her mind without forethought, and she accepted it without question. He had summoned her to him, and she would keep him safe from any danger that threatened him. Even if she still had no idea why, or what that danger might be.

Rokan took a deep breath. The directness of his gaze strengthened his resemblance to the man in the painting, though there was nothing cold or judgmental in his eyes. He was trying to appear as regal as he could, but uncertainty was written all over him, and his face was flushed from his argument with Clarisse.

"I wasn't able to wake you earlier, or I would have warned you. Nobody knows I went to the Mistwood. We think it would be best to keep your true identity a secret for now. I hope you're not offended."

"Of course not," said Isabel, who had no idea what her true identity was. "That seems wise."

Rokan ran his hand over his hair and clutched the back of his neck. "Oh. Good." He hesitated again, then blurted, "I don't actually know that much about the Shifter."

Then you know more than I do, Isabel thought, and saw an opportunity. She gave him her most enigmatic smile and said, "Tell me what you do know."

"Most of it is legend. An immortal creature who protects the kings of Samorna with her wisdom and magic." He massaged the back of his neck. "When the realm is peaceful, the Shifter sometimes leaves the castle and goes to the Mistwood. Then there may be no Shifter for twenty, fifty, once even a hundred years. But when she is needed, she always comes."

"There's even a song about you," Clarisse put in. "It's very pretty, if you like the high notes."

Isabel ignored her. Based on her brief experience, that already seemed like the best way to deal with Clarisse. She stepped closer to the door and turned sideways, so that she could be closer to Rokan without allowing Clarisse or Will out of her line of sight.

Rokan dropped his hand to his side and continued. "You left ten years ago, and at the time you were called Isabel. I was a child then, but . . ." He faltered and glanced at his sister. "We weren't sure you would come back. When you left . . . there were circumstances."

*Running through the snow, blood trailing behind her. Tears falling, not leaving a mark like the blood, and that seemed wrong. Pain. Terrible, terrible pain . . .*

"Yes," Isabel said without thinking, "there were."

Rokan straightened, pulling away from the wall. He, Will, and Clarisse looked at one another. They were afraid. Rokan and Clarisse both hid it almost well enough, but Will's face was near white.

Rokan recovered first, leaning back gingerly against the wall, trying to act casual. "So why did you leave?"

Isabel lifted her eyebrows. "I am not going to tell you that, Your Highness."

Rokan's hand tightened against his leg, but all he said was, "I understand."

Isabel highly doubted it. She changed the subject. "You were speaking of hiding my identity. How will that be possible, if people remember me from last time?"

Rokan let out a breath. "Not everyone knew who you were. For the past hundred years or so, you've always pretended to be an ordinary mortal—a sorceress, an adviser, once a nursemaid. There were always rumors, of course, but only a few people have ever known for sure."

Isabel lifted her eyebrows. "Won't there be rumors this time, too?"

"Of course, especially after your rather dramatic entrance today." He grinned at her, and Isabel's lips started to curl upward in response. Then Clarisse snorted, his smile died, and Isabel pressed her mouth into a straight line. "But we don't have to confirm them until we know . . . until you've had a chance to grow accustomed to the court." Isabel wondered if he truly thought she couldn't tell he was lying. She only wished she knew what he was lying about. "Isabel is a common enough name. We'll say you're from the Green Islands, one of those merchant's daughters whose father bought his way into the nobility. There are so many of them that no one can keep them straight."

Isabel nodded, then walked past him and Clarisse to take a seat on the plush wooden bench near the fireplace. Some of the tension had drained from the room—or from her—and she was getting tired of standing. As she sank into the cushion, though, she remembered something else. "What about the bracelet?"

The royal siblings exchanged another look she couldn't decipher. Were they afraid she was going to ask them to take it off? The bracelet felt comforting circling her wrist, the tiny, cool crystals rubbing against her skin.

"Nobody outside of the royal family knows about the Shifter's Seal," Rokan said. "It won't give you away. Many of the women at court wear jewels, so you won't stand out. I'm afraid you'll have to wear gowns, too—"

"Oh, no," Isabel said sharply. "I won't wear a skirt I can't walk in."

For a moment Rokan seemed startled. Then he laughed. "Oh, those aren't in style anymore. Women haven't worn straight skirts for years. They're all sort of—you know—flowy. Like Clarisse's."

Clarisse lifted one leg to demonstrate. Her gown was more slinky than anything else, but clearly she could move in it. Not the most practical garment for fighting in, but Isabel could manage if she had to. She nodded, careful

not to let anything but resignation show on her face.

*Don't you remember me?* Clarisse had said. If both she and Rokan had been just children when the Shifter left, Isabel couldn't possibly have recognized her on sight. But Isabel had reacted like it was a normal question, revealing how little she knew about her own past. Clarisse had smiled because she had discovered that Isabel didn't remember.

"Fine," Rokan said. He straightened, and for a moment— with his chin thrust out and his short purple cloak flung back over his doublet—he was every inch a prince. "I'm glad you're here. I want to be a good king, and you can help me. Your wisdom is legendary."

Isabel smiled thinly, wondering if Rokan had sent Clarisse to ask the question. She had been right to trust her instincts and not reveal the depths of her ignorance. Little as she knew about Rokan, she was already sure he had not called her here because he wanted guidance. If he had gone all the way to her woods on the small chance he might catch her, he'd had better reasons.

Isabel met the prince's gaze, glowing despite herself when he smiled at her. She lowered her eyes when he turned away, then raised them again to watch him go.

She didn't know who she was or what exactly she was doing here, but one thing was perfectly clear. His safety was the single most important thing in the world, and if she

had to die to protect him, she would do it without thinking twice.

But she was not a fool, and she didn't trust him one single bit.

# Chapter Three

When Isabel got to her room later that night, the high sorcerer was waiting outside her door.

She stopped several yards away from him in the dimly lit corridor. Annoyance flickered over his face as she regarded him warily, and after a second she realized why: he was invisible. She could sense the wavering outlines of the invisibility spell, like transparent flames cloaking his body, as easily as she could see him. He seemed to be a young man, but Isabel knew better; no one she had spoken to that afternoon could remember a time when he had not been high sorcerer. Nor was he particularly imposing, with a short beard and rather pudgy face. Sorcerers could make themselves handsome as easily as they could make themselves look young, but maybe in a century people got over vanity.

I didn't, Isabel thought. I cared about my hair. She pushed the thought out of her mind. The high sorcerer crossed his arms over his chest. He was wearing his formal sorcerer's robe, red and richly embroidered with a thick white stripe running down the center.

Isabel had spent the afternoon and evening circulating around the court, first in the throne room and then at the banquet that marked the end of the Challenge Days. Rokan had been right about the Shifter's legendary wisdom; her instincts had guided her unerringly to the most useful people, even in a court about which she knew nothing. Twice she had started a political argument between two people who hated each other, then faded into insignificance and listened while they became indiscreet. One of the things she had learned was that the high sorcerer was considered one of Rokan's strongest supporters, and that people were afraid of him.

What surprised her now was that *she* seemed to be afraid of him—or at least, not quite as confident as she had felt around the other members of the court. She said coolly, "Did you come here to tell me something, or—"

The high sorcerer flexed his fingers ever so slightly. A blaze of blue fire erupted from his open palm and hit her full in the face.

The fire sizzled through her, through skin and bones

and blood. It *hurt*. Lines of power zigzagged through her body, tiny explosions of pain trying to tear her apart. For a moment, just a moment, she thought it was going to work; she saw in her mind's eye how her body would dissolve, come apart into wisps of mist and fog, swirl among the shadows and be gone.

Then, abruptly, it was over. The malevolent energy burst out of her, though she had done nothing to repel it; and the magic, not her, scattered into the dim shadows of the stone walls.

Before the last blue wisps had dissipated, the high sorcerer reached into his robe and flung out his hand. The knife flew across the few yards between them. Isabel caught it by the hilt, stopping the blade inches from her eyes. Her heartbeat didn't even bother speeding up. She flipped the knife around to hold it by the blade, made a move to throw it, then tossed it to the side instead. "Anything else?"

The high sorcerer was shaking. She could hear his breath coming fast and harsh; he clearly had barely enough strength to remain standing, let alone follow up with another attack. Isabel shook her head sympathetically. "That must have been a difficult spell. How much time did it take you to create it?"

His mouth tightened. Isabel raised her eyebrows. "Oh,

was it not just *you*? How many sorcerers worked on it, and for how long?"

He said nothing, but his expression told her she was correct. Suddenly her mind was almost overwhelmed by a flood of information about sorcerers—knowledge that must have been there all along, but that she hadn't bothered to think about. She knew where the spell must have been created: at the School of Sorcery, an isolated stronghold on one of the South Sea islands where anyone with magical ability was trained and indoctrinated.

Isabel crossed her arms over her chest. "It must have taken a lot of power; it tingled a bit. What a waste of resources. You honestly thought one of your spells could work on me?"

"It did once," the high sorcerer snarled.

"What?"

"Only for a second, but *that* spell worked, didn't it? We sent you fleeing back to your woods with your tail between your legs. You're not as invulnerable as you pretend."

A sudden memory, sharp and swift. She was standing in a courtyard, in a light gray mist of rain, turning to watch an arrow fly at her from a narrow window. She reached out almost languidly to catch it. Her hand closed around the rough wood, and the arrow broke in half in her grasp; it dropped as she whirled to catch the next one, and then the next. A torrent of arrows, and she danced among them, letting them fall broken around her feet.

And then all at once her body turned to stone, refusing to obey her mind's commands. Arrested in mid-turn, she watched as the arrow she had been about to catch went right between her open fingers; a moment later she felt a sharp, tearing pain as it thudded into her side. Another arrow went past her, and another.

Isabel heard herself scream, and took a moment to realize that the sound was just the memory, that she was still standing silent as the high sorcerer smirked at her. She shoved the memory away and faced him, though the scream still beat at the inside of her clenched teeth. She would not show weakness. Not to *him*.

Not to anyone.

"Well," she said, striving to appear unconcerned, "*this* spell doesn't seem to have succeeded quite as well."

"We haven't had as much time to work on it," he growled.

"Then I suppose I'll be on my guard in twenty years." She hesitated, though probably not long enough for him to notice. She was shaken, and wanted to make her escape. But she also wanted to know what the memory meant, when it had happened, and why she had cared more about the arrows whistling past her than about the one that had pierced her side. "In the meantime," she finished, "I won't hold this against you. Know that the Shifter never disdains any assistance in protecting her prince."

*No matter how insignificant*, her tone proclaimed, and she watched the tiny clenching of nearly-invisible muscles beneath the smooth fat of his cheeks. It was a moment before he could speak, and then he couldn't manage it without spitting.

"Don't be so secure in your power, Shifter. You think Rokan trusts you—a creature without a heart, without a soul? I told him exactly what you are when he came to me for help, with his delusion that a bracelet might protect him from one such as you. I warned him what he was inviting into his castle."

"Really?" Isabel said, adopting a curious tone. "Did he take your advice?"

Albin drew himself to his full height—which was still only a few inches taller than Isabel. "He heard what I said, and he won't forget. When you eventually turn on him, he'll remember. He'll know that I was the only one who tried to protect him from you."

"How kind of you to take matters into your own hands." She moved suddenly, first kneeling to swoop up the knife, then coming to a stop only inches from the sorcerer. She was faster than any human, and Albin had no time to summon up a spell. He stumbled back several steps, and

she smiled demurely as she held the knife out to him, hilt first. "Don't worry. I won't tell Rokan about this charming demonstration of your power."

Not yet, she amended silently as the high sorcerer turned on his heel and walked down the long hall. After all, why make Albin into Rokan's enemy? Let him be hers. She, clearly, could handle him.

What made her heart pound against her ribs, so that she lay awake for a long time staring at the green canopy stretched above her bed, was the possibility of a similar attack against Rokan. Her own safety could wait until his was assured. Her own safety, in fact—she realized with neither surprise nor resentment—was of no concern at all.

Isabel spent half the next day exploring the castle; she was determined to be so familiar with it that she could walk through it blindfolded and know where every step and turn would take her. The castle was a maze of passageways and rooms and inner courtyards tiled with flagstone, halls blending into one another on most of the ground floors, upper floors crammed with narrow corridors and closed doors. She soon discovered that she had an instinctive sense for where she was, no matter how confusing the twists and turns she had taken to get there; something within her responded to a pull from the ground itself, disregarding the structures built upon it. It was a helpful sense to have.

That afternoon Rokan went to the practice ground to work on his swordplay—part of his daily routine, Isabel was pleased to learn. Today the ritual had been transformed into a semi-festive event, with all the members of the guard and a few of the nobles coming out to watch their soon-to-be king. Isabel went, too, so she could judge his skill for herself.

The practice ground was little more than a large open square between the stables and the kitchens. She was the first spectator to arrive; the only people in the square were those members of the guard who had been consigned to setting up benches to accommodate the viewers, and Rokan, who was running through some standard exercises in the center of the square. He wore loose breeches and a black silk tunic embroidered with silver threads—not, Isabel suspected, his usual practice clothes.

As she took a seat on one of the already set-up benches, he sheathed his wooden sword and walked over, plopping down next to her and leaning back on his elbows. "Are you planning to participate? Because if half of what's said about the Shifter's skill is true, your identity wouldn't stay secret for long."

"I'm just here to watch," Isabel said a bit coolly. The prospect of her prince being under attack—even fake

attack—made her tense and edgy, not in the mood for human banter. "Is that permitted?"

"Of course. Daria's going to be here, too." Rokan's face softened when he said her name, and he glanced around the square with eager eyes. "She'll arrive any minute now. You should sit with her and talk to her. After all, she may also be under your protection someday."

The prospect of spending the next hour with a demure noblewoman did nothing to alleviate Isabel's edginess. "My time would be better spent sitting with those who might pose a threat to you."

Rokan shrugged. "The guard is loyal. They wouldn't threaten me, even if they don't particularly respect me. I wouldn't worry."

"*You* wouldn't." Isabel noted the tightness around his mouth. He didn't want her talking to the guard. Why not? "But even if they are loyal, it will be useful to know my allies."

Rokan bit the side of his lip, still looking out at the square. "You need allies?"

"Did you think I would spend all my time acting as your personal bodyguard?" He blinked, and she knew that *was* what he had thought. But based on the skills she was constantly discovering she had, that couldn't be the case. "It's more subtle than that. I prefer to prevent attacks before they're launched, to dissolve conspiracies before they're formed. To help you keep Samorna in order so that there's no cause for discontent against you. I need to know everything about your allies and enemies to do that effectively."

Rokan stood, drew his wooden sword, and swung it in a slow arc above his head before moving swiftly through a series of practice slashes and parries. Isabel admired the efficient economy of his movements, though he would have appeared more graceful if his shoulders hadn't been set so stiffly. "Daria will be one of your allies."

*Spirits.* She did not have the patience for this. "I'll keep that in mind."

Rokan executed a complex series of feints, ending with an underhanded thrust, before he turned to her and rested the point of the wooden sword on the ground. "And she could use a friend."

"The other women don't like her much, do they?" Isabel leaned forward and put her elbows on her knees, trying to sound sympathetic. "They have good excuses. She's a northerner, and the southerners wish you had chosen one of them. And she's illegitimate, which insults all the highborn northern women you might have chosen instead."

Rokan's eyebrows lifted. "You figured that out in less than a day? Members of the court must be chattier than they used to be."

Isabel didn't know how chatty they used to be, but she shrugged and said, "Not really. I can learn a lot from people even when they're not talking."

He nodded, admiration clear on his face, and pride welled up in her. She was only half-bluffing; she *had* been able to learn more than she would have believed possible from her few hours at court, relying on techniques and instincts she couldn't remember acquiring. She still hadn't managed to unearth the source of the threat to Rokan, but she wasn't about to mention that to him.

"That's not all there is to it, though." Rokan rolled his head from side to side and lifted the sword again. "They didn't like her even before I began to show interest. She's different. She's not hard-edged and ruthless and manipulative like the rest of them."

Hard-edged and ruthless and manipulative. All words that applied very well to the Shifter, though Rokan didn't seem to disdain them in her. Well, one sought different qualities in a bodyguard than in a wife.

But Isabel couldn't help saying, "It can be helpful for a queen to be all those things."

"I'm not thinking about that." Rokan transferred his sword to his left hand, then back to his right. "I didn't set out to fall in love with her. Not at first. I just . . . I felt sorry for her. And the other women were so outraged when I started paying attention to her. And she was the only woman in the court who *wasn't* out to snare me so she could be queen."

Either that, or she was better at it than all the rest of them. Isabel sat up straight. "Does it matter? Last I heard, kings don't marry for love."

"I'm going to," Rokan said.

"Even if Daria—"

"I decided this long before I met Daria." Rokan thrust his jaw forward. "My parents didn't love each other. My children's parents will."

"How does Clarisse feel about that?"

Rokan rolled his eyes. "I think you can guess."

Isabel said, with a completely straight face, "I would have to draw upon all the Shifter's wisdom to do so."

Rokan chuckled. She smirked back at him, but wasn't sure what to do after that. She was vastly relieved when his dark eyes turned serious. "About Clarisse. I know she's been . . . unwelcoming to you. But she's on your side."

Her relief vanished as quickly as it had come. "Is she."

"I'm the first to admit that she can be a little difficult—"

"Really?" Isabel murmured. "The first?"

His smile came and went, very briefly, and not until it was gone did she realize she had been trying to elicit it on purpose. "All right, maybe the second or third. But it's not entirely her fault. Our father didn't treat her very well." He sat down on the bench next to her, tilting his head so he could see her better, squinting against the sunlight. "No matter what she says, though, she loves me. And I her. Even if we don't like each other very much sometimes. You can trust her."

Before Isabel could think of how to respond, a large group of guards and noblemen entered the practice grounds. Among them was Albin, accompanied by his apprentice, a dark-haired young man wearing a short red cloak. The high sorcerer scowled at them, and Isabel lifted her chin and stared back. The apprentice, unlike his master, gaped at her with wide eyes.

Rokan got to his feet. He hefted his sword, bowed to her with a wry grin, and walked out into the square.

Today's practice consisted of a series of matches between Rokan and the guards. After several tense minutes, Isabel realized that not only were none of Rokan's opponents going to threaten him with serious harm, they were all going to great lengths to make sure he won. She could tell by the suppressed mirth in Rokan's eyes that he knew it, too.

Once she was sure enough of his safety to relax, Isabel turned her attention to Daria. The object of Rokan's affections was medium height and slender, with soft brown hair and softer brown eyes, and she spent the entire practice session watching Rokan with breathless attention. She wasn't the type of girl men were usually smitten with—you had to watch her for a while before you noticed how pretty she was—but that, Isabel supposed, was Rokan's business. There was an air of straightforward sweetness to her, a sincerity devoid of intensity, that might hold great appeal to someone raised in a swirl of courtly intrigue.

"He's completely smitten," said a voice on Isabel's right, and she turned sharply to stare at the speaker: a foppish young nobleman with an elaborate lace collar that he obviously, and mistakenly, thought made him look dignified. By his lilting accent, he was from the south. "If you were hoping to make a try for our prince yourself, I'm afraid you're out of luck."

Isabel stopped herself just in time from giving him her deadliest glare. Instead, she pouted. "I've heard people say the match is ill-advised."

"Oh, it is; no doubt about that. If the king were alive, it wouldn't be happening." The nobleman bit his lip and lowered his voice, a pattern Isabel had noticed before. Everyone seemed reluctant to talk about Rokan's father. The few times Isabel had brought him up, people had slipped away from her and found someone else to talk to, even when that required a break in the smooth finesse so prized among courtiers. "Samorna needs southern trade more than it needs northern armies. The prince should be seeking his wife among the southern noblewomen."

Wood thudded on wood behind her. Isabel started to turn around, then realized that she didn't have to. She could feel the air bouncing off swords and bodies behind her, allowing her to draw an accurate image in her head of every person in the practice ground. She felt rather than saw Rokan sheathe his sword and bow to the guard he had defeated. The discovery startled her so much that she nearly forgot to uphold her end of the conversation. "Er—the northern dukes tend to be more difficult, don't they?"

"Nothing new about that. They like to think of themselves as honorable and loyal subjects"—he rolled his eyes—"but I believe history has shown them to be more protective of their own privileges than of their king's honor. In any case, Prince Rokan isn't going to make them any less troublesome by marrying some noblewoman's by-blow."

Isabel simpered. "Well. Maybe his mind can be changed."

"You think so?" The nobleman eyed her skeptically, which Isabel supposed would have been insulting if this were her true form. She smiled at him, and something in her smile made him turn his attention suddenly to the new round of sword fighting about to begin.

\* \* \*

Later that night Isabel made her way to Clarisse's suite and knocked loudly on the door.

She was surprised when Clarisse opened the door herself. The princess was wearing a long, clingy dressing gown and reeked of perfume. She stared groggily at Isabel without quite focusing on her. Isabel hadn't seen Clarisse at the evening's banquet, but there had certainly been wine enough there to explain the princess's state.

Then Clarisse blinked, and her eyebrows slanted downward over suddenly hard green eyes. "What do you want?"

Isabel had prepared herself for coy, faked politeness. She dropped that idea hastily. "I want to talk to you."

"You can't," Clarisse said, and began to close the door.

Isabel stretched out one arm and shoved the door open. The princess staggered back a few steps as Isabel walked in.

She saw at once why Clarisse had opened the door herself. The room was empty, with not a single maidservant to help the princess dress or pull her bed drapes closed before she slept. Isabel could not have been more shocked if she had found Clarisse living in squalor. But the room was large and grand, and cluttered with so many expensive chairs and tables that there was no straight line of space that went more than two yards.

Clarisse crossed her arms over her chest, and Isabel followed suit. Clarisse was the person most likely to know the source of the threat to Rokan—the threat that nobody else seemed to know about but that had sent him riding after a legend to seek protection. The challenge lay in getting that answer without letting the princess know she needed help. Fortunately, Clarisse had just handed her an excellent place to begin.

"I'm mildly curious," Isabel said, "to know why you hate me."

Clarisse's scowl lifted. "I'm a bitter, hateful person," she said in an almost friendly tone. "I hate everybody." She took two steps back and sank onto a plush chair, keeping her eyes on Isabel the whole time.

"You don't hate Rokan," Isabel pointed out.

"Are you serious? Of course I hate Rokan."

"I see. Is that why you hate me—because I'm here to help him?"

Clarisse began to look away. Then she snapped her head back and said, suddenly and sharply, "*Is* that why you're here?"

Impasse.

*I don't know.* Isabel almost said it. Instead she raised one eyebrow and said, "Why do *you* think I'm here?"

Clarisse considered her for a long moment, then lifted a

slender hand to her mouth and stifled a yawn. "What did you want to talk to me about, Shifter?"

"I have a name."

"Do you have any objection to my calling you 'Shifter'?"

No answer she gave to that could be right. Isabel took a deep breath, feeling something close to panic. This conversation was already spinning out of her control. Or rather, Clarisse was pulling it out of her control. She was very good at it.

Isabel should have been better.

The silence stretched, and every passing second was a point in Clarisse's favor. Finally the princess yawned, stretched, and put her arms on the armrests of her chair.

"If you're going to stay there and stare at me," she said sweetly, "why don't you do it sitting down? It's much more comfortable."

Isabel forced herself to take the three steps toward the closest chair, and even then she couldn't bring herself to sit. For a moment she thought of a deer backed into a hard spot by wolves, turning in panic with nowhere left to run. The idea felt familiar; she could almost smell the wolves and hear their low, panting breaths. But something about the memory—if that was what it was—felt wrong.

Clarisse looked her up and down and smiled, the assured smile of a predator. "All right, *Isabel*. You came here in the middle of the night to talk to me. I assume it's important."

Isabel attempted a haughty chuckle. "It's not quite the middle of the night, Clarisse."

"Maybe not to you, but it's pretty late for humans."

Isabel had enough control to keep even a flicker of emotion from crossing her face, and Clarisse stretched her arms overhead. "I'm tired," she said, "so if you have anything to say, I suggest you hurry up and say it."

Isabel realized suddenly why the image of the deer felt wrong. She had been there, but not as a deer. She had been one of the wolves.

Blood pulsed through her with the memory, laced with the thrill of the chase. She took two quick strides forward and grabbed Clarisse's arm, jerking her up from the chair. She was surprised to find Clarisse ready for that, braced against it—but the princess's resistance made no difference. Isabel pulled her up effortlessly.

In a voice like ice, Isabel said, "I came here to ask you who's trying to kill your brother."

There was a short pause. Clarisse's mouth tightened, but instead of another snide remark, she said, "Is someone trying to kill him?"

"I believe so," Isabel lied. "I thought we might work together to find out who."

Clarisse pulled her arm away, and Isabel let her do it. The princess's cold green eyes were only inches away from hers. "Sorry. You're on your own. I wouldn't dream of getting in your way."

"Have you heard any rumors—"

"*Completely* on your own."

"Why?" Isabel said.

Clarisse took two steps back, but she didn't turn, and she didn't take her eyes off Isabel. "How many people get the chance to watch the Shifter at work? I couldn't possibly pass up the opportunity. It's going to be absolutely fascinating."

"Sure of me, aren't you?"

"The Shifter is a legend." Clarisse rubbed her arm where Isabel had grabbed it. "Although I'm beginning to wonder why. You're blundering already, giving too much away, making too many assumptions."

Her words hurt, because they were true. As steadily as she could, Isabel said, "Like what?"

Clarisse turned her back. "Like assuming I would want an assassination attempt stopped."

Isabel laughed, and Clarisse swung back around to face her. "You think I'm not serious?"

"If you were serious," Isabel told her, "you would never be stupid enough to say it in front of me. I'm sworn

to protect him, and I could kill you right now."

"Why? I'm not a direct threat. I wouldn't plot to kill him myself." Clarisse sat on the same chair, her expression daring Isabel to pull her up again. "But maybe I wouldn't mind if someone else did it for me."

Isabel stepped closer, arm muscles clenching. Clarisse pressed herself against the back of the chair, but didn't lower her eyes. "I'm not going to help you. I want to have as little to do with you as possible. And I always get what I want. So why don't you go do something useful? Shift into a cat or something and—"

"Shift into a cat?" Isabel repeated.

Clarisse sneered. "What's the matter—did you forget how?"

She had forgotten that she was able to. Isabel stood still as a statue, cursing herself for being so stupid. What had she thought *Shifter* meant? No wonder the prince was willing to rely on a slip of a girl for his protection, when that girl could at a moment's notice take the form of a tiger or a wolf.

Sudden confused memories flooded her mind—air streaming beneath her wings, warm flesh dying between her jaws, earth sliding around her scales. Living with an immediacy that deepened every moment.

Isabel focused on Clarisse, who was watching her with

51

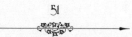

faint suspicion. Suspicion of what? With an effort, Isabel smiled.

"It's not something you forget, Princess. It's what I am." *What I am, and I didn't even remember it.* "I meant—why a cat?"

Clarisse shrugged. "It's said the Shifter preferred the shape of a cat."

"I *am* the Shifter," Isabel said, the memories going straight to her mouth without touching her mind. "I know what I did." She leaned forward. "And I didn't prefer the shape of a cat. I just wanted everyone to think I did."

Clarisse blinked, and suddenly Isabel had the upper hand. She turned toward the door. "I'll leave in human form. But I might not return that way—and you'll never know, will you?"

"I knew Rokan shouldn't have brought you here," Clarisse spat at her back. "You'll be his ruin."

Isabel turned her head. "Don't make me laugh, Princess. You're not worried about Rokan. You're afraid I'll be your ruin."

There was a moment of silence. Then Clarisse said, her voice unreadable, "Will you be?"

Something in her tone caught at Isabel. She almost said, "Not if you don't stand in my way." But she remembered

who she was, and what she was here for. Not to make friends, and not to be kind. Keeping Clarisse off balance was the best way to deal with her for now.

"I might," she said. Then she left Clarisse's room and made her way through the corridors to her own.

The decorated walls and ornate furniture seemed alien to her, closing her in, obstructing her freedom to move. She went to a window and pushed the heavy green drapes aside. Beyond the courtyard, invisible in the darkness, black mountains rolled across the horizon in gentle waves. Her bedroom was on one of the highest floors of the castle, but a bird could fly right out into the cool night. She closed her eyes and tried to shift her shape.

No, she didn't. She tried to *try*. She didn't have the faintest idea of how to begin. She formed the image of a bird in her mind and tried to will herself into it. She thought of her legs changing, shriveling, her arms flattening into wings and growing feathers. She gave up on the intermediate steps and simply willed the change into being.

Nothing.

After some time—she couldn't have said how long—she stood back from the window, feeling as if someone had dropped iron bars over it. She stepped sideways and stood before the mirror. Her hair had reverted to a slightly frizzy reddish brown, as it did whenever she wasn't paying

attention. Maybe the Shifter's instincts were telling her to be inconspicuous. But it was too late—the Lady Isabel had gleaming blond tresses. She raised her hands and brushed them over her head. When they dropped back to her sides, her hair was golden again.

She couldn't have said how she did it. She just did. She leaned closer to the mirror and closed her eyes. When she opened them, they were emerald green, so bright it was clearly not natural. Isabel frowned, and the color softened.

Then she touched her chin and tried to make it more rounded.

Nothing. After a full minute of intense concentration, her face was still the same, sharp-jawed and thin. Isabel swore.

Changing colors was minor, a magic most sorcerers could manage. She had to be capable of more than that. She was called *Shifter.*

She closed her eyes and tried again. Maybe a bird was beyond her powers—but then why did she remember flying? She thought of a wolf, a cat, a deer, and tried and tried and tried. When she finally threw herself onto her bed in exhaustion, her body was drenched with sweat.

She fell asleep instantly and dreamed of soaring above the treetops, of racing through the snow with the scent of blood in her nostrils, of sliding her long, cold body around

a rock. She woke up with her blankets thrown off her bed, her hands throttling her pillow.

When was the last time she had shifted? The prince had found her in human form, but she hadn't known he was coming. Why had she been human? For how long had she been human?

The body she wore seemed to wrap around her, stifling her, trapping her into the limited movements of which it was capable. She wanted to fly. She wanted to run for days without tiring, to have muscles that could wrestle prey to the ground.

What was wrong with her?

She thought she knew who could answer that question. Rokan had known where to find her, what to say to her, had known to clasp the Shifter's bracelet around her wrist. She had determined not to trust him, not to let him see any weakness, but now she needed answers too badly to care. Her loyalty was to him, anyhow. If she could not protect him as well as he expected her to, he had a right to know.

Her room was lit faintly with rosy light, and the air blowing in through the still-open window was cold. It wasn't much past dawn, but she couldn't wait. Rokan would be in the king's bedchamber, and without even having to think about it, she knew exactly where that was.

* * *

When the door to his room creaked, Rokan sat up instantly in bed, his skin tingling. He had stayed up late last night, waiting for that very creak, and had finally gone to sleep miserable with disappointment. The invitation he had given Daria had been clear enough, though couched in courtly hints, and the look in her eyes had made him hope she would take him up on it. He had even left his bed curtains undrawn and given his guards orders to let a woman through. But she hadn't come.

It was early morning now, but they wouldn't be disturbed; the chamber between his room and the hall was empty but for two guards. His father had gotten rid of all the people who attended the king in the morning, announcing to the startled courtiers that he was partial to pissing and dressing all by himself. That was one decree Rokan had no intention of rethinking. So maybe . . .

Rokan's heartbeat quickened when he saw a slim figure slip through the door and turn to close it. But even before she turned to face him, he knew who she was. She moved with smooth, powerful grace, without a single wasted motion.

He arranged his features into what he hoped was a friendly expression. "Hello, Isabel. What are you doing here?"

"I came to talk to you." She walked over to his bed and pulled herself up onto the foot of it, apparently seeing

no impropriety in the act. The light filtering in through the window let him see the outlines of her face, and he spent a moment eyeing the strange, dangerous creature he had resurrected. In a yellow gown, with her golden hair spilling down her back, she could have been an ordinary noblewoman . . . almost. Something in the way she held her head, the way her eyes darted around the room, made him wonder how it was the entire court didn't know that a wild creature walked among them.

"I'm sorry," the Shifter said. "You were expecting somebody else."

How had she—of course. The guards. Rokan cursed his fair skin as he blushed. "Not anymore I wasn't," he lied.

The Shifter tilted her head, and her eyes caught the moonlight. She didn't say anything. She didn't have to.

Rokan's face was on fire. He reminded himself that she wasn't a person, and wouldn't care. "All right. I was still waiting for her. But she's not coming."

"That's all quite obvious," Isabel said, amused.

"Oh, good. Because I was getting bored of having a sense of self-respect." Rokan pulled himself straight and rested his shoulders against the polished wooden headboard. It was obviously too late to act regal, but he did his best. "I was not expecting you, either."

Those green eyes were wide now, but no less feral; the

neat line of lashes framing them looked out of place. Too human. "I want some answers."

Rokan's heart thudded almost painfully, but he merely inclined his head. He had been expecting this. He still hadn't decided how much to tell her. "What do you want to know?"

"I want to know why you brought me here."

The way she said it, it sounded like a challenge. Rokan forced his face, his voice, to stay calm. He wished Clarisse was there. "Why is the Shifter ever here? I need your protection."

"You don't seem to be in danger, Your High— Your Majesty."

"I can't be called 'Majesty' yet," Rokan said. "Not until my coronation, in another sixty days." Her lips tightened impatiently, and he stopped stalling. "But yes, in truth I was king the moment the Challenge Days ended. And I am in danger."

"If you are," Isabel said, leaning forward, "then no one at court is aware of it."

He resisted the urge to lean away from her. Instead he held himself carefully upright, letting his shoulders slouch so he wouldn't seem tense. "It is possible to keep things from the court."

"Not for long."

"No," Rokan admitted, "not for long." He hesitated, biting his lip. "Besides, the court may know. It keeps secrets better now than the last time you were here. My—my father was a harsh king. People learned to be wary."

She nodded. Rokan spent a moment trying to decipher her expression, then gave up and continued. "Some of the legends say that the Shifter's memory fades every time she retreats to her woods, so she returns with few specific memories of the last king she served. Is that true?"

"Yes," Isabel said.

He pursed his lips so he couldn't smile. "So you don't know the circumstances under which you left last time?"

"No." Her fingers dug into the bedspread, but aside from that slight movement, her body was as still as a hunting cat's. "Do you?"

"Not really." Suddenly there was no reason to be afraid of her—for the moment, anyhow. Rokan felt almost giddy. "I was only seven years old at the time. There was some sort of attempt on the king's life, and you disappeared right afterward. Some said you fled from shame. I don't know of what."

"Neither do I." Isabel's voice was intense, but not threatening. She believed him.

Recklessly, Rokan elaborated. "Some say you swore never to return. I was warned against trying to find you.

But I need you. My enemies haven't actually made an assassination attempt yet, but they will. And I don't know where it will come from. I don't know who they are or what they want."

"Then how do you know they exist?" Isabel asked.

Rokan met her eyes. This next part was inspired. "The high sorcerer told me."

"The high sorcerer," she repeated slowly.

"He was here when . . . when you were. He's very old, nobody knows how old, but he's been at court for at least a century. He cast an oracle, and it told him there was someone who would try to have me dead before my first year as king was out."

She stiffened. Watching her, the way her muscles tensed and her whole face went focused, Rokan was once again certain he had done the right thing in riding to the Mistwood. His guards and advisers were useless, but she would keep him safe. She was smart and strong and fierce, and she would stop at nothing.

The hidden, gut-tightening fear he had been living with for days eased slightly. He was able to keep his voice expressionless. "I thought you might be able to protect me."

"Of course I'll be able to protect you," Isabel said almost absently. "Excuse me."

She turned and left, pausing in the doorway to glance

back at him. She looked like a deer poised for flight, her slim body taut in the incongruous gown, her face sharp and still. Then she turned and was gone, and Rokan dropped back onto his pillows, limp with relief. She was going to do it. She was going to watch over him. Best of all, his biggest worry had just ceased to exist. She didn't remember what had happened last time, the real reason she had fled to her woods.

*Of course I'll be able to protect you.*

She never would have said that if she remembered.

# Chapter Four

*I should have told him.* The two guards in the outer chamber watched her go, probably curious but too well-trained to show it, and Isabel forced her face to reveal nothing. She could still feel, like a fist around her heart, the fear in her prince's voice. Still see the hope in his eyes as they rested on her face. He thought he had ridden into the Mistwood and brought back a magical beast, a shape-shifter who could take his fear away. Her presence made him less afraid. She didn't want to take that away from him.

*Even so. I should have told him.*

The castle was dimly lit this early in the morning, making it difficult to see where she was going in the windowless passageway. Isabel had not noticed that on the way to Rokan's room. She wondered how she had missed it when suddenly, for no apparent reason, it was no longer difficult.

She stopped, peering ahead down the corridor and then back over her shoulder. There was no light. The corridor was as dark as it had been a moment ago. But she could see it clearly.

She lifted her fingers, touched her lower lashes briefly, and blinked. Again, it was dark. She shifted her eyes back, and—like a cat—she could see.

Interesting.

Without any real hope, she tried shifting her entire body into a cat, Clarisse's taunt humming in her ears: *It's said the Shifter preferred the shape of a cat.* She gave up after a few seconds, not wanting to ruin the sudden euphoria that had sprung up in her. She wondered if her eyes were elongated and slitted, but there was no mirror in which she could check.

Did this mean she was regaining her powers? Or had she been able to do this all along, and hadn't noticed?

Either way, it would make protecting Rokan easier. Maybe in a few days she would be able to shift. Maybe it was normal for the Shifter to return with faded memories and faded powers, and regain them slowly as she served her king.

A sudden memory shot through her like pain. Running through the snow. Blood falling. And all around her, through her, *in* her, the bitter knowledge of failure.

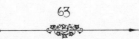

The euphoria vanished, and Isabel bit her lip so hard she tasted blood. *Failure.* For a moment she knew where she had been running and why, and she knew the reason for the failure. Then the knowledge was gone.

*There were circumstances,* Rokan had said.

It shouldn't matter. She should focus on her goal. Locate the threat to Rokan, and get rid of it.

Even if he was still lying to her about the source of the threat.

*The high sorcerer told me,* Rokan had said, looking her straight in the eye. *He cast an oracle.*

But that was a little too convenient. Rokan must know how the high sorcerer felt about her; must know that Albin would never help her in any way. And maybe that was *why* he was claiming the mysterious warning had come from Albin; because he didn't want her to know where it had truly come from.

*He came to me for help, with his delusion that a bracelet might protect him,* Albin had said. Obviously, Albin would never have lifted a finger to bring the Shifter back. But Rokan had ridden to the Mistwood anyhow, carrying the Shifter's Seal. He must have received assistance from someone else.

Isabel considered for a moment, then turned around and went back the way she had come.

A few twists and turns brought her to one of the spiral staircases that wound its way through the castle. The high sorcerer's workroom was at the top of the staircase, and the scent of potions leaking down from it was so strong that, even at this distance, Isabel had to fight an urge to flee.

She forced herself forward—not up the stairs, but onto the landing that branched away from them. The heavy wooden door at its end gave way easily to lock-picking skills she hadn't realized she possessed. She was rather pleased with herself as she pushed the door open.

The sorcerer's apprentice was waiting for her, which dimmed her pleasure somewhat. She had thought she was being soundless and had expected the advantage of surprise. But the dark-haired young man was standing with his back against a large wooden table, watching her without a hint of fear.

No fear . . . but no antagonism, either, that Isabel could detect. She shifted her face expressionless and gave herself a moment to adjust to the feel of magic and to survey the room for possible dangers. It was sparsely furnished: a bed crammed into one corner, a wooden table covered with a jumble of copper candlesticks, inkwells, and quills, and a glass-covered bookcase stuffed with leather-bound volumes. The arched white ceiling was blackened, and the rush matting near the table had been burned through to reveal the oak boards beneath.

Isabel had until now seen the apprentice, a young man named Ven, only from a distance. Up close, he had a dark, broad-cheeked face and blue eyes that contrasted sharply with thick black eyebrows. Isabel tried to imagine how a normal human girl would react upon encountering such a face, and settled on a stunned expression. That should cover most eventualities.

"I'm sorry," she said, testing his reaction. "I didn't know . . . that is, I seem to be lost."

Without moving, he said, "I know who you are."

Isabel went still. Even though she had expected him to know—and hoped he knew far more than that—her body reacted to his words as if to a threat. Just in case, she said, "You do? Are you acquainted with my parents?"

His lips twitched upward. "Your parents are the wind and the fog, according to several songs. I don't think they meant it literally, though."

For a moment they stood and stared at each other, while Isabel considered her options. She finally chose a tone threatening enough to warn him, but not enough to frighten him off. "So you know."

Suddenly his face was no longer opaque; his expression was all eagerness, like a child's. "I'm not the only one who knows. The whole court is wondering. But they didn't think the Shifter would come to Rokan."

Why not? Isabel thought, but she didn't say it. She relaxed slightly. His eyes gave him away—they were still fiercely intent on her, but not in the wary, aggressive way Albin watched her. They were filled with incredulous wonder. She stepped into the room.

"You're the high sorcerer's apprentice," she said in a flat tone that he could interpret however he liked.

"I know he hates you," Ven said. "I don't share his views. He doesn't understand anything about you. I've studied you for years. I know much more about you than he does."

Or than I do, Isabel thought. This was better than she had expected. "Why didn't the court think the Shifter would come? Doesn't she . . . don't I always come?"

Ven shrugged. "You used to. At least, that's what they say. But it's been so long since you used your powers in public that already some people are saying you never existed. Others don't deny that there was someone called the Shifter—a bodyguard, assassin, completely loyal—who guarded the king. But they say you were simply a well-trained sorceress. They say the legend was built around you deliberately."

"Interesting," Isabel said, leaning back against the door frame.

He swallowed a grin. "I never believed it, of course. And there *are* a few people who remember seeing you shift. The royal cook told me you used to come to him in the shape of a cat to eat scraps of meat. Is that true?"

It seemed unlikely. "Yes," Isabel said with a grave nod. "That's always been a habit of mine."

Ven rose up slightly on the balls of his feet. Isabel got the distinct impression that if he hadn't been trying to act dignified, he would have jumped up and down. "I knew it! When you're a cat, you have a cat's instincts as well as its form. I never met a cat who could resist handouts."

Did she have a cat's instincts? Isabel held herself still, but if she had been as uncontrolled as Ven was, she would have jumped up and down, too. He would spill information like a sieve if she handled him right. "How do you know that?"

"I've been collecting the pieces of your legend for years. I came to apprentice in Samorna because here is where you've lived and fought and protected for all these hundreds of years. They have all these books about you . . . and now I'm actually talking to you. It's almost unbelievable."

It was almost embarrassing, was what it was. Isabel said nothing, and Ven rose up slightly again. "You will talk to me, won't you? I want to study you." He stopped, apparently realizing how tactlessly that had been put, then

forged ahead. "You retain the habits of your past guard-
ianships? So you're really one person, not a succession of
different ones? Not person, I mean—of course you're not
human—but I'm babbling." He flushed and flashed a hopeful grin. "You'll let me study you, won't you? Please?"

Isabel's instinct was to say no. She bit that back and let
a long moment pass before answering. "Maybe. If you can
offer me something in return."

Ven settled back to the ground and chewed the side of
his lip. "What do you want?"

"Tell me why Rokan came to get me. What danger does
he want my protection from?"

He put his hands down on the table behind him, and
his eyes skittered away from hers. Isabel advanced into the
room, sliding one foot in front of the other with a stealthy
predator's grace. She watched with satisfaction when he
leaned away from her, wishing he could flee. She gave him
a moment to realize he couldn't.

"I know he came to you for help first," she said when she
was only a few yards away from him.

Ven's knuckles were white against the scratched wood
of the table. "He—he did come to me. But he never told me
the specific reason he was seeking you out."

"Didn't he?" She let her eyes change color, from green
to black, while he was looking at them.

Ven drew in his breath sharply. With an obvious effort, he let go of the table and stepped toward her. "He didn't. But I can guess. I know why he might be in danger, and why you weren't already here to protect him from it. Not just why you're here, but why you *left*."

Isabel's muscles suddenly felt too tight. "What makes you think I don't already know?"

"I know Rokan was hoping you wouldn't remember. He asked Albin for assistance before he decided to go find you, but Albin refused. So Rokan came to me, and he told me what happened last time."

She closed the distance between them and grabbed his wrist, squeezing hard enough to cause pain. "*Tell me.* Why did I leave?"

"It might be treason," he blurted. He didn't even try to pull away from her, though she could feel the strength in his arm. The legend was serving her well.

"It might," she agreed, and waited.

Ven closed his eyes briefly, like a man preparing to jump off a cliff. "You left after you tried to kill Rokan's father."

# Chapter Five

*Blood. On her hands, dripping to the floor, soaking the arrow she wrenched out of her side as she ran from the courtyard. She could taste it, choking her. . . .*

The memory struck with brutal force, making her gasp. It was gone in a second, leaving only the feeling of pain and guilt and fear. *Fear.* She had been afraid.

"That's not possible," Isabel said, trying to focus on Ven. It was too late to pretend his statement had not come as a shock. "The Shifter—*I*—can't allow a member of the royal family to die, let alone kill one."

He braced himself and said, "Rokan's father wasn't the king."

"What do you mean?"

"He was the captain of the castle guards. He organized

a rebellion and killed the old king and his children."

Isabel let his arm go.

To her surprise, Ven did not step away from her. "The School of Sorcery had secretly been working for decades on a spell that could affect the Shifter. Albin provided it to Rokan's father. They had been working on the spell for fifty years, and it managed to hold you for about five seconds. Long enough."

The arrows flying past her had been aimed at her king. Isabel's chest hurt.

"You tried to kill Rokan's father, but he told you his soldiers were on their way to execute the king's children. By the time you managed to reach the children, it was too late—they were too securely trapped, and you couldn't save them, either. You fled from shame. It was said that if you ever came back, it would be for vengeance."

"Vengeance," Isabel repeated numbly. It didn't strike the slightest chord. None of this did; it might as well have happened to someone else. "Vengeance is a human conceit."

"I suppose it is," Ven said. "That's why we assume you would want it. That's why no one has guessed who you are. No one can believe Rokan would be foolish enough to go searching for you, no matter how uncertain his reign. Odds were you'd kill him, not protect him. He had no way to know you would accept him as the new king."

"He had the bracelet," Isabel said.

After a barely perceptible pause, Ven said, "Yes. He did have that."

"Didn't he realize I would find out?" Isabel said.

"During Rokan's father's reign, it was a crime punishable by death to speak of the coup. People are still afraid, and they still don't talk." Ven finally stepped back, but this time it wasn't from fear; when he rested against the table again, his arms were loose and relaxed. "Besides, according to legend, the Shifter doesn't think about things that don't matter. Once you accepted Rokan as your charge, it wouldn't matter to you who his father was. Even if you learned the truth, you might just . . . not acknowledge it."

Was that true? Isabel wondered. Did she not think about things that didn't matter? If she *was* thinking about it, did that mean it *did* matter? "Sounds a bit like wishful thinking to me," she observed.

Ven flushed, and Isabel wondered why—Rokan's wishful thinking was hardly his fault. "Yes, well. They realized it might not work that way. That's why Rokan had me track down the bracelet. Once you accepted it from him, it would keep you from harming him."

"Then why didn't he tell me the truth?"

Ven stretched his legs out in front of him. "Maybe he thought if you spent some time protecting him before

73

you realized the truth, it would have a better chance of working. And you do want to protect him, don't you?"

"Yes."

"From the start?"

No. Not until after she had scratched his face. Not until he had fastened the bracelet around her wrist. But she had let him fasten it, hadn't she? And this was something Ven had no way of finding out. "Yes. It was immediate."

"How odd." Ven frowned slightly. "And interesting. Maybe with all the members of the last dynasty gone, your loyalty switched instantly to the new one."

What kind of loyalty was *that*? But it could be true, if she had been bound to protect the kingdom itself, to maintain a strong monarchy no matter what.

"I can find out," Ven said eagerly, straightening. "You'll let me, won't you? I have dozens of books, everything ever written about the Shifter. And spells, and lore . . . I'll find out why you're reacting the way you are."

It would be dangerous, because he *was* Albin's apprentice—but if he could help her figure out what had happened to her, and to the powers Rokan was relying upon, it would be well worth the risk.

"All right," Isabel said slowly, exuding reluctance.

Ven tried to nod gravely but could not repress his grin. "I'll see you tomorrow, then? At dawn?"

Isabel nodded and turned her back on him before she could give in to the urge to grin back.

She wasn't sure, as she continued down the stairs, whether she had the answer to her original question. If Rokan's reign was the result of a decade-old coup, his right to rule was open to question in a way no Samornian king's had been for centuries. He certainly had reason to seek out extra protection. But why choose a form of protection that was just as likely to turn on him?

Whatever his reasons, he had gambled correctly. She was on his side. Despite what she now knew, every part of her yearned to wipe away the fear she had seen in his eyes, to ease the tension that seemed always a part of him. And she was the Shifter. Her instincts were infallible.

Should be infallible.

What would happen to the Shifter if there was no one left for her to protect? Would she drift apart, back to fog and wind, with no more reason to exist? Would she find something else to do?

Or someone else to protect?

She went to Ven's room the next morning, and every morning after that. She didn't have to push much to get him to talk about her; she was all he wanted to talk about. And it was reassuring, in a way, to listen to him go on endlessly about the exploits of the Shifter—tales he had read or been told or heard in song. In the past, it seemed, she had been all-knowing and nearly all-powerful. His stories tweaked memories that made it easy for her to pretend she still was, and to believe she would be again.

The only thing he ever asked her was whether the tales were true. She told him they all were, even the most wildly implausible ones, and he never doubted her. His awe grew daily.

She spent the rest of each day at court, gathering information she could use to advise, and impress, Rokan. Her store of knowledge became more solid with every fragment and nuance. Sometimes her memory would surprise her with sudden spurts of information—about the growing threat of the Raellian Empire, or the long-standing enmity between two northern dukes, or the intricacies of the Green Islands trade routes. But she couldn't control when that happened, so she couldn't rely on it. What she could depend on, it soon became clear, was her ability to ferret out secrets with frightening efficiency.

On the fourth day, she went to meet Rokan in his bedchamber. He had asked for the meeting—until then, he had been too busy to do more than occasionally exchange a few sentences with her—and Isabel's anticipation grew as the morning dragged on.

But Rokan wasn't in his bedchamber when she got there.

This was the first time she had seen his room in the daylight; it was decorated much like her own, but in maroon and gold rather than green, with tables scattered among the ornate chairs. The tapestry to the right of the bed portrayed a stormy sea, all dark blue shadows and white waves and a horizon that melted into the sky. Isabel had never seen a tapestry quite like it. She studied it for a moment before turning to the guard who had half-risen from one of the polished wooden chairs along the wall.

"Er," the guard said. "The prince—His Highness asked me to tell you to meet him in the stable yard. He said he prefers—"

Isabel was gone before the guard had a chance to finish the sentence, racing through the hall and down the stairs so fast her feet never seemed to touch the ground. She had a vague impression of shocked faces turning to watch her and knew she was moving faster than any human could have run, but she didn't care. Her heartbeat was pounding even faster than her footsteps. If this was some sort of trap—if Rokan *wasn't* in the stable yard—

Someone shouted a command as she flew past. He was behind her, so she couldn't tell who it was—and then, suddenly, she could: a castle guard, his sword half-drawn.

There was no way peripheral vision could extend that far backward, so her eyes must have actually shifted position in her head. She snapped her focus back to the corridor ahead of her.

A long, narrow set of stairs led down to the stables; when she reached them, she threw herself into the air. For a few breathless moments she hung suspended in midair, her leap carrying her out over the stairs; then she fell like a stone and landed on her feet only inches past the bottom step. She used the impact to catapult herself into the stable yard.

Rokan was mounted on a gray gelding, and a stable hand held the reins of a brown mare. Both horses startled as Isabel came to an abrupt stop; Rokan's gelding reared, and the prince had to twist to keep from being thrown. Isabel nickered at the horse, an exact echo of the sound a stallion would use to calm a fractious mare. The gelding came back down, snorted, and stood still.

Isabel crossed the large flat stones of the yard, and the stable hand let go of the mare's reins in his haste to get away from her. One quick glance told Isabel he wasn't a threat; his fear was all of her, and she could hardly blame him for that. She grabbed the mare's reins before they had finished swinging and pulled herself into the saddle.

"Next time you decide on a change of plans," she told Rokan, "you should tell me about it yourself."

"Right," Rokan said faintly. "I'll keep that in mind."

"Do that." Isabel turned the mare around in a tight circle, alert for dangers she might have missed. The stable yard was a narrow rectangle surrounded by the wooden stables on three sides, empty but for Rokan, herself, and the terrified stable hand. A moment later the guard rushed down the stairs, but stopped short at the sight of the two of them mounted. "And why *are* we changing our plans?"

"Because it has occurred to me that though it's no longer safe for me to go riding alone, it's probably safe to go riding with *you*."

Isabel glanced over at the stable hand, but Rokan had pitched his voice low enough so the boy wouldn't overhear. "Why do you need to go riding at all?"

Rokan grinned at her sideways. "If I spend one more second inside the castle, I may go mad. Insane kings are notoriously bad for their countries. So it's your duty to indulge me in this."

"I wouldn't care if you were bad for your country," Isabel said, and was surprised when Rokan's smile dimmed. Had she implied something without intending to? "Although insane kings are probably also difficult to protect."

"Yes. Clarisse makes that point to me often." The smile was back, making his eyes gleam. Rokan had the type of face that became long and angular when he smiled, but the way his eyes came alive more than made up for it. "Usually when I want to go riding, in fact."

"Well, she's right." Much as it annoyed Isabel to say it.

Rokan turned his horse toward the gate. "Once, when I was younger, I broke out of a formal procession and rode straight out that gate. No one saw it coming in time to stop me. I galloped directly away from the city gates for an hour before I came to my senses." His grin didn't fade even as he added, "My father had me beaten to within an inch of my life."

"You put yourself in danger." Isabel's sympathies were with his father.

The grin did disappear then. "That's not why he did it. I had embarrassed him." He leaned forward and stroked his horse's neck. The gelding snorted and pulled at the reins. "My father did not like being embarrassed."

"Your father sounds like . . . quite a man."

Rokan shrugged. "Kingship requires such men. So he always said."

"You don't agree?"

A lock of dark hair fell over Rokan's forehead, and he didn't bother to push it away as he straightened in the saddle. "I don't know. I guess I'll find out how much like him I have to be."

Isabel remembered the portrait, the cold, judgmental

gaze. She regarded Rokan through half-shut eyes. "Or how much like him you *can* be. I think you'll find it's not very much at all."

"Thank you," Rokan said, then blushed and laughed at the same time. "Sorry. You didn't mean that as a compliment, did you? My father outwitted all his many enemies and ended up dying of a natural infection. I'm sure you wish I was more like him."

"No," Isabel said without thinking.

He raised his eyebrows, waiting for her to explain. Isabel had no explanation, so she spurred her horse toward the gate.

They rode in silence through the steep narrow streets of the capital city, past crowded houses of weathered stone and iron rails. Isabel did not like the city. There were few open spaces and fewer trees, and even the sky was blocked by the vastness of the northern mountain range. There were too many potential hiding places from which an enemy could spring.

It wasn't until they had left the city behind and turned toward the flat lands to the south that she relaxed enough to begin talking again. "You rode alone when you came to find me, didn't you? Will wouldn't be much of a protector."

Rokan, too, had relaxed once the city was behind him, swaying easily from side to side as he adjusted to the gelding's changing gait. "There was no choice. Only members of the royal family may enter the Mistwood. The villagers tell some rather grisly stories about what happens to people who disregard that rule."

"Do they," Isabel said, and bared her teeth savagely. But her heart wasn't in it. She hadn't even known Rokan was *in* her woods, not until shortly before he found her. Clearly, the villagers were wrong.

She wondered how much of the lore surrounding her *was* wrong. Perhaps she had built up much of her own legend deliberately, to make her task easier. Maybe that was the problem now: she was trying to live up to her own lies.

The Shifter, it turned out, was not a great rider. Presumably it wasn't a particularly useful skill for a creature who could be a horse herself if she chose. Isabel was fine when the mare walked, cantered, and even trotted; in fact, she rather enjoyed watching the mountainous terrain flattening into gentle hillsides, the grass bending ahead of the wind in dark green waves. Far ahead she could see trees beginning to dot the hillside, and the breeze that stirred her hair made her skin tingle. She could feel mist on that breeze, as faint as a whispered breath. The Mistwood was still hours of riding away, but she knew where that mist came from. It made her feel like she *was* the legend, like she could shift just by wishing it. It was enough to make up for the discomfort of riding.

But Rokan, it soon became apparent, liked to gallop. He liked to gallop really, really fast.

After the third time he had to wait for her to catch up, she shifted her breathing steady and said, "I would prefer that you not do that. I have enough trouble protecting you from others without worrying that you're going to kill yourself accidentally."

Rokan laughed, his hair in windblown tangles, his face alive with pure exhilaration. "Don't worry about it, then. I'm an excellent rider."

"I can't help worrying about you. It's part of what I am." He smiled even more widely at that, and she said repressively, "Besides, it wouldn't matter how good you were if someone had sabotaged your saddle. Did you even check the saddle girths?"

Rokan's grin died, replaced by an expression of concern—which had been her goal, so there was no reason for a pang of regret. "No." And then, challengingly: "Did you?"

"I would have been able to tell by the way your horse moved if there was any problem."

"Well, see? That's why I brought you along." Rokan smiled, but it was a regretful smile that brought no light to his eyes.

A piercing cry sounded above them, a cry that sounded eerily like a human scream. They both looked up to watch a hawk spiraling upward in the air, higher and higher. A sharp pain ran through Isabel as she watched the dark shape against the blue sky; she had a sudden memory of soaring, of wings spread to catch an updraft, of folding those wings for the heart-stopping drop on unsuspecting prey. She imagined the edges of her body blurring, forming feathers to lift her off the earth.

"Spirits," Rokan breathed, and she felt an almost physical thud as she was pulled back to earth—or back into her body—though since the horse beneath her didn't stir, it must have been only in her mind. "What does it feel like to fly?"

"It feels free," Isabel said.

Rokan turned his head and smiled at her—an astonishingly wide-open smile that transformed his face, stripping away any hint of seriousness, his eyes alight with wonder. Isabel jerked her gaze back to the sky, a sudden energy tingling through her. The hawk let out another sharp, piercing cry. That cry, combined with the spread of wings and the way it wheeled across the sky, formed a message: *Danger. Human danger.*

Isabel dismounted and knelt in one smooth movement. She pressed her hand against the grass, pushing at the dirt beneath it, closing her eyes. Subtle reverberations ran through the ground, and some part of her was able to pull out the ones she cared about, to know what they meant. A heavy weight,

over the hills to the south. Stomping hooves. A horse.

Someone was watching the road to the Mistood. Waiting.

Isabel got to her feet and snapped her eyes open to find Rokan watching her, dark eyes wide, the way a man might watch a glorious sunset or the crashing sea. She felt alive with power, completely nonhuman; her skin might swirl away into mist at any moment.

"We have to go," she said. There was nothing human about her voice, though it formed human words, and Rokan's fingers tightened on the reins.

"Why?"

"This isn't safe."

Rokan was instantly tense, alert, and afraid. His hand moved to the hilt of his dagger. "What do you want to do?"

"I want," Isabel said, swinging back onto her horse, "to go back to the castle. Now."

They got back in half the time it had taken them to ride out. And this time she had no trouble with the galloping at all.

On the sixth morning, on her way up the tower stairs, Isabel met Albin coming down.

They froze for a moment, the sorcerer in his thick red robe that reeked of old potions, Isabel in a pale violet gown with her golden hair tied up in braids. Then the door to

Ven's workroom opened, and the apprentice stopped short on the threshold, all the blood draining from his face.

Isabel gave Ven a coldly impersonal look, then turned back to Albin. "I'm here to ask your apprentice some questions. I would advise you not to interfere."

Albin drew himself up. "I don't take advice from a creature like you."

"Call it a warning, then."

His face hardened, and Isabel realized that she had miscalculated. She hadn't thought he would be foolish enough to once again test his strength against hers. But she hadn't taken into account his reluctance to lose face in front of his apprentice.

She reached into her flowing sleeve for the dagger she now carried strapped to her arm. With her eyes on Albin, she pulled out the dagger and threw it sideways—not at Albin, but at Ven.

Albin would have been prepared with a magical defense. Ven only flinched and gasped, and the dagger thudded into the half-open door inches from his throat. Isabel had not looked at Ven when she threw the dagger, and she didn't now. Instead she kept her eyes on Albin. "If I intended to hurt him, it would not be difficult. I'm merely doing what I was summoned here to do. I need some information about the prince's magical protection."

The implication—that she couldn't force the information from *him* just as easily—would please Albin. Isabel
waited a moment, then added, "I can have Prince Rokan
order him to talk to me, if that would make this easier for
you."

Albin made a great show of deliberating, then jabbed his
finger at Ven and scowled. "Answer her questions. But take
care. She is an unnatural creature, with no human feelings,
and the kings of Samorna are fools to believe they know
her purpose. Don't be swayed by her delicate form, and
don't make the mistake of trusting her for a second."

Ven managed a nod. Albin fixed Isabel with another
glare, then swept past them down the stairs.

Ven took a deep breath and touched the hilt of the still-
quivering dagger, his hand shaking.

"I'll need that back," Isabel said.

"You could have—"

"Killed you?" Isabel cocked her head to the side, allowing herself a small chuckle. "I don't miss."

"No . . . of course not." He took another breath, and
the fear faded from his face, overshadowed by the awe she
had grown used to—and started to enjoy—over the past few
days. She smiled at him, and he grinned sheepishly back. Her
smile wasn't all calculation, either. There was something . . .
easy . . . about being with Ven. She would have said she

enjoyed his company, if such a thing were possible.

*No human feelings.* Not being human herself, she couldn't assess the truth of that. But she was fairly sure the Shifter didn't feel a need to relax, or to be admired by anyone other than her prince. And wouldn't enjoy either of those things. She spent time with Ven purely because he was useful to her.

"Well," she said, "Albin will want to know what my questions were. We should review what you're going to tell him."

Ven nodded, turned, and went back into his room. As she followed, Isabel pulled the dagger out of the door and slid it back inside her sleeve. It left a deep narrow gash in the dark wood, which would serve as a nice reminder for Albin every time he walked up these stairs to his room. Inhuman or not, Isabel allowed herself a brief, smug smile before she shut the door behind her.

# Chapter Six

When the attack came, it was completely unexpected.

Rokan had been thinking it would be a relief. He was thinking it at the moment it happened—sitting on the dais with a goblet of wine in his hand, watching the dancers step delicately around one another at yet another of the endless banquets, frustrated because he couldn't get caught up in the light-headed giddiness that was overtaking everyone else.

The room was crowded and well-lit by late afternoon sunlight, the scent of wine so thick it weighed on the air, laughter floating through the music. Everyone was flushed, everyone was laughing and eating, everyone but him. The danger pressed on him, weighing him down. Parties like these made him remember how effortless it had once been

to forget his cares, and how impossible it was now.

Not everyone was dancing. The Shifter stood near the wall, as still as a statue, her gaze flitting around the room. He watched her eyes move from a group of ambassadors in furious discussion . . . to a pair of dancers who had announced their betrothal that morning . . . to a serving boy who had just dropped a platter of roast fowl . . . to a cluster of richly dressed northern dukes murmuring too quietly for others to hear. Back in his father's day not one of them would have dared even murmur—except for Duke Owain, too high-minded to learn stealth, but Owain wasn't here. He had excused himself from tonight's banquet due to a mild illness, leaving his niece unchaperoned. For all the good that did Rokan.

Still, the thought of Daria lifted his spirits a little. He started to look for her, and at that exact moment he heard her scream.

The dancing and the music took a few seconds to stop, and by that time the screaming had stopped, too. Rokan surged to his feet, trying to see through the crowd. A woman started shrieking and was joined by another. They were backing away from a spot on the floor.

Rokan's heart stopped. Without remembering how he had gotten there, he pushed through the crowd, rudely shoving a duchess aside, barely able to think about how Daria's scream had been sliced off in the middle. He stepped between the two shrieking noblewomen—they went abruptly silent when they saw him—and stared at the place near the wall where Daria must have been standing.

Some glass shards lay on the thin gray rug, surrounded by rose-colored wine. Otherwise, nothing.

He turned to call the Shifter and saw that she was right behind him, her face calm but her eyes darting to the glass and the wine, then to the people all around. With her was the sorcerer's apprentice, but not the sorcerer.

"What happened?" Rokan demanded.

One of the noblewomen answered him. "She was standing there, talking to me, and then she screamed, and then—then she was gone. Like magic!"

*Like* magic, indeed. The lady was a minor noblewoman from a seaside duchy, someone Daria couldn't stand and would never have spoken to for more than a second. The jostling for position never stopped, even at a time like this. "Where's Albin?" Rokan heard his voice rise and forced it into a semblance of rationality. "Where did they go?"

Isabel lifted her eyebrows slightly and glanced at the apprentice. "Ven? What can you do?"

The young man darted forward, knelt, and dipped his finger in the fast-disappearing wine. "I can track her. It will take a few minutes—"

"Then start now!" Rokan shouted.

Someone touched his wrist. Clarisse was standing at his side, two castle guards behind her. "Rokan, you have to calm down."

He shook her off, suddenly aware of the reason for her warning—the mob of faces surrounding them, watching him, judging how he reacted to a crisis. He did not want to be aware of them. For a moment he hated his sister. "I don't know what happened to her! I don't know where she is or—"

"She's in the castle," the sorcerer's apprentice said. He stood, his brow creased. "I can take you to her."

"Rokan—" Clarisse said warningly.

"You stay here," Rokan snapped at her. "Explain things." There was nothing to explain, but Clarisse would manage anyhow. "I'm going. The guards will stay here and make sure nobody leaves."

"You can't go yourself—"

"I'll go with him," Isabel said almost dangerously, and Clarisse's protest died on her lips. "Come on."

They took off at a run. The apprentice was too slow, and Rokan almost yelled at him before he realized that he was concentrating hard as he ran. His breath came in short hisses.

"Ven?" Isabel said. "Do you know where you're going?"

"I'll know when I— There!" The apprentice came to a

panting stop in the west hall, an almost unused corridor lined with rooms, with a few faded tapestries and a bare stone floor. A lock of hair flopped against his forehead, soaked with sweat. "That room. Over there."

"That's just an empty bedroom," Rokan said, and started toward it. Then he jerked to a stop.

Isabel was holding his wrist. She stared at him, those eerie green eyes calm, her rose-colored gown stripping the wildness from her, making her appear ordinary and frail. But her grip was like steel.

He didn't bother trying to break it. He inserted every ounce of command he possessed into his voice. "Let—me—go."

"It seems clear," Isabel said, "that this is a trap."

"She's in there!"

"I know."

"She could die."

"I know." The grip, impossibly, tightened. "So could you."

"I have to go in after her."

"No."

"*Isabel.*" He did try to break her grip then, an effort as futile as he had known it would be. He slammed the side of his hand down on her arm, and she didn't even flinch. Her arm looked like flesh but felt like stone. The glittering bracelet dangled on her delicate wrist.

The bracelet . . . it was worth a try. Anything was worth a try. Even though the hall was silent, Daria's scream echoed in his head. "Shifter," he snapped, "by the power I have over you, by the bracelet I gave you, by the Shifter's Seal you took from me—*let go of my hand.*"

Her fingers opened slowly, reluctantly, peeling away from his wrist. He backed away from her, unable to believe it had actually worked. "Stay here."

She shook her head angrily. "I *will* protect you, like it or not. I don't have a choice. And you—you are the king of Samorna. You have no right to die."

"I don't plan to die."

"You have no right to risk it. This is what they expected—that you would act like a reckless child. They want you, not her. It's your responsibility not to walk into their hands."

"Sorry, Isabel, but I'm human, and I do have a choice."

"Then make the right choice!"

He turned away from her and snapped, "Ven!"

Ven raised his hand. The door burst, taking half the wall with it.

Daria sat on a plush chair near the bare bed, her hands bound behind her back, her dark hair half piled on her head and half straggling down her face. She let out a sob and screamed, "Rokan!"

"Don't!" the Shifter shouted, but it was too late. He was already moving forward. He saw Daria smile, but even if he had understood what it meant in time, he was moving far too fast to stop.

When Ven raised his hand, Isabel felt a sizzle run down her spine. She saw the door splinter apart in slow motion, and knew what Rokan was going to do as soon as she saw Daria. Without thinking, she sprinted past him through the remains of the doorway.

A movement at the corner of her eye. A scent. She turned to face it just as a heaving mass of fur and teeth hit her in the chest.

She went over backward, the creature on top of her, her heart pounding—not with fear, but with shock at the thought that she had almost let the prince go in, that it could have been Rokan the beast attacked. He would have been dead by now. The creature's teeth had closed over her neck the second it hit—but she had been ready, some animal instinct from when *she* had hunted, and her neck had turned to stone. The thing had hurt its teeth and now sprang away from her with a furious yowl.

Snowcat. Another shock. The size of a small horse, deadly at the best of times, worse when it was scared. Nothing could fight a snowcat—

—except another snowcat, Isabel thought, and grinned fiercely as the beast sprang.

But there was no snowcat to meet it; there was only a slim blond girl who had forgotten about the powers she didn't have. Expecting to be a cat, she had half-risen to meet the creature, growling. By the time she realized, it was too late for any of the tricks she *could* manage. She landed on her back with the cat on top of her, its hot breath blasting into her face. A claw ripped open the side of her arm, trailing such fiery pain that she screamed and raised her other arm to push it off. Curved teeth tore through her forearm.

*It will go after Rokan next.* She shifted her legs, making them stronger than humanly possible, and kicked. The snowcat yowled in surprise as it tumbled halfway across the room, but it landed on its feet. It crouched, heavy muscles rippling beneath white fur, and snarled at her.

She shifted her arms, ignored the pain that lingered even though the wounds were gone, and jumped to her feet. It was a leap that would have been impossible for a human, but at the time it was instinctive. She landed right in front of the cat, so fast it had no time to react. One quick step sideways, another leap, and she was on its back, her stone-like arm wrapped around its neck and pressing against the jugular.

The snowcat went mad, twisting, biting, scratching. She held on, shifting grimly and swiftly, repairing each gash and bite and scratch. The cat rolled, trying to crush her; her body went stone for a second, long enough to live and hang on, not long enough to avoid pain. The pain was a problem. She could feel the burning scratches, the ripped muscles, the crushed bone even after they were no longer there.

She held on, and after what seemed like forever the cat was still, a bloody mass of hot fur. Most of the blood was hers. She got to her feet, shifting the last of her wounds away, shifting her hair and skin at the same time. Cool, impassive—with the same unruffled expression she wore at court functions—she strode away from the huge cat's corpse. Beneath the bloodstained gashes in her gown, her skin was white and smooth. She was the Shifter, and everything hurt, but nothing would show.

She had just fought a snowcat and won.

*Who cares? I've probably* been *a snowcat.* But she couldn't help the flush of triumph that went through her. She turned to Rokan.

Rokan was gone.

Ven stared back at her through the ruins of the doorway. There should have been awe in his eyes, but instead there was something else . . . something she didn't recognize and didn't want to analyze. She hesitated, then blurted, "Where is he?"

"He went to see if he could catch Albin," Ven said. He, too, was cool and unruffled.

"Catch—" But she realized before she finished asking the question. Only magic could have brought the snowcat here and kept it docile until the right moment. Cats were notoriously difficult to manipulate with sorcery. It would have taken powerful magic.

Albin must have thought that even the Shifter might lose to a snowcat. Underestimating her again. She couldn't summon up even the faintest hint of smugness.

"Albin knows spells that could have taken him halfway across the world by now," Ven said. "But I guess Rokan had to try."

Still not liking the expression on his face, Isabel turned away from him and started toward Daria. Who was also gone.

"Spirits!" Isabel snapped. "When—"

"Just now." Ven's voice was still infuriatingly calm. "He must have taken her. Fairly dangerous spell, that, even when the person you're taking is cooperating with you."

*Cooperating with you.* It had not been a kidnapping. Daria hadn't shouted a warning, even when Rokan had been about to walk in and the cat had been about to spring.

"Spirits," she said again, more softly. "He really loved her."

Ven shrugged. "Do you worry about the king's feelings, or only his life?"

"Not all dangers are obvious," Isabel said randomly. She had no idea what it meant, but it sounded good, and Ven was beginning to annoy her. And he was still watching her. She snapped, "What?"

"You didn't shift."

Long pause.

"I didn't have to."

"So?"

"So why should I?"

"Why shouldn't you?"

Talking in circles had its uses. It had given her time to come up with an answer. "I didn't want Daria to see."

Ven's eyes went so narrow she could no longer see their blue. "I saw your face when the cat leaped. You didn't have time to take that into account."

"*You* wouldn't have had time. I did." Isabel tried her enigmatic smile, despite a sinking feeling that it wasn't going to work this time.

Ven said nothing. He merely stared at her for several seconds—a long, hard stare, clearly not liking what he was seeing.

Isabel stared back, fairly sure that her expression was the same.

# Chapter Seven

Isabel caught up with Rokan halfway down the stairs, on a dimly lit landing with a tiny window cut into the thick stone wall. The guards from the ballroom had finally made it halfway *up* the stairs, and the landing was a confused mass of frightened, sweaty, panting people. Rokan was shouting at the guards to let him through, and though half of them were trying to obey, the other half were trying to reason with him. When Isabel leaped onto the stair above the landing, Rokan was drawing his sword.

She reached around him and grabbed the sword by its blade, shifting her hands to stone as they closed around the sharp edges. She pulled the sword from Rokan's grasp so deftly that he didn't at first realize what had happened. He stared at his empty clenched fist, then whirled around.

Isabel flipped the sword into the air and caught it by the hilt. A few of the nearer guards flinched or ducked, but Rokan stood right where he was and glared at her.

"It's probably not a good idea," Isabel said, "to draw a weapon on your own guards."

"I have to find Albin!"

"And you think he went back to the ballroom?"

"I need to get to Clarisse—"

"Clarisse can't help you. Albin could be anywhere by now." Interesting, the difference between humans and Shifters; the same rage that made Rokan's eyes blaze like coals was turning her into ice. She met his gaze without flinching. "If you want to find out what happened, you need to focus on the people still within your reach. Have your soldiers arrest Owain."

He swallowed hard, turned, and issued a few short orders to the guards. In addition to arresting Owain, he told them to seal off the castle and organize a manhunt; wasted efforts, but Isabel didn't try to stop him. By the time he finished and turned back to face her, he sounded almost coherent.

Isabel handed back his sword. He took it and sheathed it without ever moving his eyes from her face. They were wide and bewildered. Isabel's heart lurched. This was a hurt it was too late to protect him from, a hurt beyond the Shifter's ability to salve.

Beneath her sympathy, though, she was angry. Daria was someone Rokan had chosen to love, and even before her betrayal, she hadn't been worthy of it. If humans were going to care so deeply, they should be more careful about whom they decided to spend their affections on.

"Isabel—" Rokan began, and his voice cracked. "I should have—"

Yes, you should have, she thought fiercely, but she didn't say it. She wasn't angry at Rokan—or at least, she shouldn't be. She should have watched Daria more closely. If she was what she was supposed to be, she would have stopped this before it happened.

"Go find Clarisse," she said. "I'll make sure Ven is trying to discover how Albin did it. Once Owain is in custody and you've calmed the court, we'll meet in the south gardens."

For another moment Rokan stood there, his hand still on the sword's hilt. Then he took a deep breath and set his shoulders. "Right," he said, and turned to the remaining guards. "Two of you with me. The rest go ahead and make sure the way to the ballroom is clear. Let's go." The guards exchanged glances, and he raised his voice—just a notch, but it was enough to make them scramble to obey. "*Now.*"

He looked back at Isabel. "Why the garden?"

"Albin wouldn't expect us to meet outdoors now that

it's grown colder. He won't have set up any spells there."

Rokan nodded. "I'll be there, then."

Isabel let a smile touch her lips but go no further. She bowed her head briefly. "As will I, my prince."

Ven was one step ahead of her. By the time Isabel reached the room where the snowcat's corpse lay stretched across the floor, he was already working a spell. She stopped in the doorway and watched him.

Ven stood with his eyes closed, swaying unsteadily on his feet. The air around him was full of shimmering translucent colors, like sunlight seen through lowered eyelashes, patternless and beautiful and threatening all at once.

Ven drew in his breath and opened his eyes, and the colors vanished. Isabel steeled herself for the expression on his face.

But Ven merely shook his head and said, "I can't find him, Isabel. I'm sorry."

"Do you know how he did it?"

"Yes."

"Then that will have to do. Come with me."

She was glad of the excuse to turn away, but when he stumbled into step next to her she regarded him more closely. His mouth was slightly slack, and his eyes seemed to have a hard time focusing.

Isabel surprised herself with a rush of real concern. "That spell wasn't easy for you, was it?"

"No spells are easy." He tried to smile but gave up halfway through the effort. "Better sorcerers can push the effects off longer, that's all."

He staggered, and she reached out and took his arm, closing her hand around the silk of his sleeve. He froze for a moment; then he kept walking, his arm heavy on hers. "We don't understand magic at all. We can only use it, and even that only barely. It's not meant for us. It takes great concentration to twist the human mind into a vessel that magic can flow through. And to actually direct that flow—" He shook his head. His hair was flat and limp, his voice so low and labored that Isabel had to shift her hearing to make out his words. "All these—the potions, the chants, the spells—none of them have any effect on the magic itself. They work on our minds. Force them into unnatural shapes so they can do unnatural things. It's different for you—you *are* magic, in your very essence. I can't imagine what that's like."

The wonder in his voice was a welcome salve to the doubt she had sensed in him earlier. Yet human magic had made it past her watch tonight, just as it had ten years ago.

The Shifter did not use spells; they were designed for human minds. But she had never feared them, either, because she knew she could block any spell directed at her charge. That was why the spell tonight hadn't been directed at her prince, or the spell years ago at her king; she would have seen those coming and stopped them in time. She had been too focused on protecting them, if such a thing were possible. She had never imagined that anyone would strike at her.

She felt icy cold. It was better when they pushed through a wooden door out into the gardens, where a few autumn flowers bloomed stubbornly among mostly leafless bushes. Her skin and blood shifted in response to the cold, so subtly that even Ven, whose arm was resting heavily on her hand, didn't seem to notice. Not that he was in a position to notice much. As soon as they neared a wooden bench, he went for it and dropped like a stone, leaning his head back and closing his eyes.

"It's so cold," he said absently, making no move to wrap his arms around himself.

Isabel scanned the area around them, every sense alert. Medium-sized flower bushes, mostly bare at this time of year, were scattered among trees and saplings. Tiny streams curved among artful rock formations, filling the garden with the sound of gurgling water. The autumn flowers—and, she suddenly knew, the spring and summer ones as well—had subtle, almost spicy smells, nothing overwhelming. There was no space in the garden she couldn't see or sense, no way anyone could sneak up on them. She wondered if she'd had a hand in designing the garden.

"Why did Albin do it?" she said. "He helped Rokan's father with the coup. He has nothing to gain by turning on Rokan now."

"Loyalty doesn't figure much into his decisions," Ven said, eyes still closed. "He must think the northern dukes will treat him better than Rokan would, just as he thought Rokan's father would treat him better than the old king. Although that didn't work out as well as he'd expected. He and Rokan's father had a falling out only a year after the coup."

Isabel sat next to him. "Why?"

"Rokan's father hired a rogue sorcerer for additional protection. Albin wasn't happy, even though he kept his title."

A rogue sorcerer. Usually far more powerful than trained sorcerers, but that was mostly because they didn't know the safe limits of their powers. "What happened to him?"

Ven forced his eyes open. "She died three years ago. Lost control of a spell and vanished in a spurt of white flame. They found pieces of her all over the castle."

He sounded much less self-righteous about it than a

proper sorcerer should have. Isabel was willing to bet he hadn't been the star pupil at the School of Sorcery, no matter how talented he was. She was about to say something about that, trying to think of something worth the energy it would take Ven to laugh, when she caught a scent on the chill breeze and turned.

Rokan and Clarisse were deep in discussion, blond curls and dark head bent together as they walked down the winding path. They stopped a few feet away, right by a small stream that curved over polished rocks in a series of tiny waterfalls. Isabel approved; the steady rushing sound would mask their conversation even if Albin had planted some sort of listening spell here. It would also fill up any awkward silences. For a long minute none of them said a word.

"There's no sign of Albin," Clarisse said finally. Talking to Ven, not Isabel. Ven blinked at her, eyes glazed. "Or of Daria."

Isabel glanced quickly at Rokan, but if his expression changed, she missed it. He might have been posing for the statue he would have made of himself one day. Cool, commanding, and absolutely without emotion. The waterfall gurgled as Clarisse went on. "Her uncle is in custody. He claims he doesn't know anything."

"Let me question him," Isabel said grimly. "I'll find out what he knows."

"That doesn't seem called for," Rokan said. His voice was like his face, even and controlled. "I don't think he would tell us anything under torture—certainly not the truth. Albin is the one we want—he would break under the mere threat of torture—but he's out of our reach."

"I never did like that man," Clarisse muttered. She sat on the bench on the other side of Ven, using one hand to sweep her skirt around her legs and away from the ground, and shot a malicious look at Isabel. "No one with that much power is reliable, no matter how loyal they claim to be."

Isabel kept her face blank. "The high sorcerer," she said evenly, "is out of our reach for now. The duke is not."

Rokan shook his head. His movements were short and jerky, not controlled at all, though his voice was still steady. "There's no point. And he's probably innocent. Imprisoning or executing him will only give the other dukes a cause to rally around, and torturing him won't give us any information. I'm going to release him. I'm sure he'll head obediently back to his duchy and try not to call any more attention to himself."

There was a tinge of casual scorn in his voice, more like a habit than a deliberate inflection. Clarisse noticed Isabel noticing, and she smirked. "Our father did not think highly of Duke Owain."

"He's a fine man," Rokan said, but the scorn was still there. "Just not capable of coming up with a scheme like this. He thinks in straight lines."

For no particular reason, Isabel thought of the portrait in the audience chamber, the grim face and uncompromising eyes. She was sure she was hearing that man's voice now, coming out of Rokan's mouth.

"It was Albin's idea," Clarisse agreed, and scowled at Ven. "Though you seemed to recover from the shock fairly quickly. Did you suspect what he was going to do?"

Even in his stupor, Ven sensed the danger in that question. He straightened and focused on her. "No! Of course not."

"Don't be ridiculous," Isabel snapped. "He helped us, didn't he?"

Clarisse leaned back. "Led my brother straight into the trap, you mean?"

Ven tried to say something, but he obviously couldn't formulate a coherent sentence. Isabel felt a rush of rage. Clarisse was only doing this because Ven was such an easy target, weak and crippled prey.

"You should go," Isabel said to Ven.

He turned toward her, clearly struggling to think. Fear darkened his eyes, and it took her a moment to realize that it was her he was afraid of. That hurt, though it shouldn't have. If he had played a part in Albin's plot, she would kill him without a second thought.

Wouldn't she?

"Go," she said again, more gently.

He nodded and stumbled away down the path. Clarisse twisted to watch him, then whipped back toward Isabel.

Isabel met her glare straight on. "He didn't know anything."

Clarisse's lips curved in triumph. "Are you sure? Is that what you've been doing with him all week? Finding out what he knows?"

"What's your point, Clarisse?"

"I think it's odd, that's all. And suspicious."

"You're suspicious of *me*?"

The princess's eyebrows arched. "I'm not questioning your motives. But maybe your judgment is clouded."

A small cascade of pebbles sprayed out suddenly from under Rokan's boot. He turned on his sister almost savagely. "By what? His blue eyes and high cheekbones? Not everybody is *you*."

Clarisse blinked, her lips parting. It took her only a second to recover. "I'm merely pointing out—"

"You're merely spouting idiocy," Rokan snapped. His heel made a small crunching sound as it dug further into

the ground. "She's not a human being, Clarisse. She doesn't *get* blinded by emotions!"

The silence that followed was long and raw, and the murmur of water did nothing to fill it. Rokan's cheeks were red. When he spoke again, his voice was stiff. "I think we're done for the day. I'll see you both tomorrow."

Neither Isabel nor Clarisse said a word as they watched him leave. Then Clarisse brushed off her skirt and said, "I don't get blinded by cheekbones. I just enjoy them. Not the same thing."

"He wasn't really talking about you."

"I know. But I don't like the way he talks about *you*." Clarisse put both her hands flat on the bench, pressing down so hard her fingertips turned white. "He thinks you're infallible."

So he did. So he should. But when he'd said *She's not a human being*, it hadn't sounded like a compliment.

"That's probably because I am," Isabel said.

"You didn't see this coming, did you?"

Isabel flinched, and was furious at herself for it. "Rokan's a lot smarter than you give him credit for. Why don't you just trust his judgment?"

"You know what I think?" The tip of Clarisse's slipper drew short, sharp lines in the gravel. "I think he brought you here simply because he felt like it. Such a romantic legend, such an ancient tradition. Rokan likes romantic legends."

A romantic little boy, Albin had called him; Clarisse, it seemed, shared the high sorcerer's opinion of her brother. Isabel thought they were both wrong. But perhaps it was no bad thing for them to go on thinking it.

"Is that such a terrible trait?" she said.

Clarisse laughed. Something in the laugh made Isabel shift her sense of smell, but she still couldn't make out any wine on Clarisse's breath.

"I don't believe in legends," Clarisse said, "and I don't believe in tradition. It's tradition that makes Rokan king instead of me, even though I was born first."

Isabel had been about to get up to follow Rokan. Instead she turned and watched Clarisse carefully from under lowered eyelids. "Do you hate him for that?"

Clarisse gave a small, tight smile, and Isabel knew that her casual manner hadn't fooled the princess. "Wouldn't you?"

Isabel didn't answer. The question touched something inside her, something she couldn't identify and didn't have time to. Instead she said, "It's not his fault."

"No," Clarisse said bitterly, "not *his* fault. But it doesn't change the way things are." She rested her elbows on her knees. "Do you know that I never spoke to my father?"

"Excuse me?"

Clarisse shrugged. "I saw him at state affairs, when I was invited to attend. I spoke formal words in court. But I never once talked to him. Not so much as 'I want a new dress' or 'Rokan hit me.' He took me from my mother so she could get busy producing a son, and I was raised by court officials and tutors. It's not the sort of upbringing that makes you believe in romance and legends. Or in much of anything."

Isabel hooked her finger around her bracelet, rubbing the smooth crystals between her finger and thumb. "And Rokan—"

"Rokan was raised by court officials, too. But my father had time for *him*. Oh, yes. He was the heir. He had to be trained and molded."

Isabel remembered what Ven had told her about the king's ruling techniques and said, "I don't think he molded him quite the way he intended."

"No." Clarisse laughed shortly. "Rokan was a stubborn brat when he was a child, even worse than he is now. But the point is that he loved my father. He might disagree with him, he might disapprove of him, but he loved him. That's where people get their respect for tradition, isn't it? From loving their parents? I guess that's why Rokan has it and I don't. It's why he rode out to get you even when I told him it was the worst idea he had ever had."

"That," Isabel said, "and the fact that he's a stubborn brat."

She actually surprised a smile out of Clarisse. "That goes without saying. But the point, Isabel, is that I'm what you might call a realist, and Rokan is not. That's why I'm so much better at protecting him than he is at protecting himself."

"Are you?" Isabel said in as neutral a tone as she could manage.

"Oh, he can fight and ride and all that—my father made sure of it. But he never sees danger until it's right in front of his face. He's not afraid of anything." Clarisse laughed without humor. "So I'm afraid of everything, to make up for it."

Isabel just looked at her.

"I'm usually right," Clarisse added. She tilted her head slightly to one side, making her hair tumble over her shoulder in a riotous wave. "But of course, you would know that, wouldn't you?"

For once it was not a challenge. She was offering an alliance.

Isabel was dangerously tempted. In some ways Clarisse was better at this than she was; it shouldn't have been possible, but it was true. Clarisse knew more about Rokan,

and more about Albin. She was better at confusing people. Isabel could use Clarisse.

Or Clarisse could use her.

The temptation faded, leaving a faint tinge of regret behind. It was too risky. She didn't understand the princess at all; didn't understand her motives, her goals, the contradictions in what she said and in the ways she acted. There was no way Isabel could control Clarisse.

"You advised Rokan not to come get me," Isabel said sweetly. "So you're not always right, are you?"

Clarisse considered her for a moment. Then one corner of her mouth twisted upward, her cheek dimpling in what was almost a smile. "I think," she said as she stood, "that that remains to be seen."

Isabel watched Clarisse walk away. It was entirely possible, she thought as she rose from the bench, that she had just made her biggest mistake since the moment she let Rokan fasten that bracelet around her wrist.

Will was waiting in Rokan's room, pouting because he hadn't been invited to talk with him and Clarisse. Rokan stopped in the doorway, almost more afraid than he had been when he first saw the snowcat. But there was no disappointment in Will's eyes, only anger.

"I liked her," Will said.

Rokan clenched his jaw. When he spoke, he made not the slightest effort to control his voice and was surprised when it emerged steady anyhow. He was learning to be a king.

"I thought I knew her. I saw what I wanted to see, I suppose. I fooled myself."

"She fooled you," Will said. "She's not a bad actress, is she?"

"No. She's not. I didn't even think she was capable of telling a lie. . . ." His voice wavered there a bit. *Careful, Rokan.*

Someone coughed, and he turned to see the Shifter standing behind him. She was still wearing her tattered rose-colored gown, slashed into barely decent pieces by the snowcat meant for him. Her skin beneath the strips of fabric was whole and clean, though he had seen her flesh torn into ribbons. Her eyes were wide and intent, watching him.

It felt like a reproach. Rokan took a step back and said, "I'm not you, Isabel. I'm human, and I believed what I wanted to believe. I didn't want to be alone. I wanted her to love me."

She blinked. Will, unhelpfully, said, "Clarisse didn't like Daria."

"Clarisse doesn't like anyone," Rokan snapped. "She

didn't understand Daria, that was all. They were too different."

"I guess she understood her better than you," Will said.

His tone wasn't accusing, or sharp, but Rokan's breath caught. He gave his brother a slow, sideways look. Will was grimacing slightly, but the expression was for Daria, not for him.

Rokan exhaled. It had to happen eventually, he knew. One day Will would look at him the way he had once looked at his father. The hero worship would drain from his eyes, and in its absence would come hate—hate because he wasn't a hero, wasn't worthy of worship. Sooner or later it would happen.

But not today. He couldn't bear it today. Not right after the way Daria had looked at him, in that second before she vanished.

He faced the Shifter again. She would see him the same way for a hundred years, if he lived that long. He was not a person to her, only a king. For once he welcomed that. "Will, you should go."

His brother scurried out of the room, giving the Shifter a wide berth. Isabel didn't even acknowledge him as he passed. "Do you think Albin will try again?" she said.

It was a stupid question. Not really a question, then—merely a way of opening the conversation. "I don't know.

I don't want—" He took a deep breath and stepped back again. "I don't want to talk about it now. All right?"

"He could strike at any time. We have to—"

"Please."

She studied him for a moment. Her eyes were dark now, like the snowcat's, cool and opaque. He wondered if she felt sorry for him, or if she was simply assessing his ability to handle Daria's betrayal. Did the Shifter like him? Or did she just have to protect him?

It was stupid to care whether she liked him. Daria hadn't liked him. She had merely had to spend time with him until the trap was sprung. Perhaps duty was the most he could expect from anyone.

"All right," Isabel said finally. "We'll talk about it tomorrow."

She turned and strode from the room, the shredded garment swaying around her calves and ankles. Rokan gripped his right hand with his left, squeezing until it seemed there must be no blood left in either. Safe, he thought, before realizing how ridiculous that was. If nothing else, this night had proven that he was safer with the Shifter around than without her.

Cold comfort. He put out the lamps and sat in darkness for a long time before he fell asleep.

# Chapter Eight

In her room, surrounded by green, Isabel went straight to a window and threw the drapes open. Cold air rushed in, hitting her skin and sweeping back her hair, raising goose bumps on her arms. She leaned out and stared at the courtyard far below.

If she jumped, would that do it? Would she turn into a bird in mid-fall, if she had no other choice? She gripped the edge of the sill until her knuckles were white, leaning out so far that all it would take was a loss of balance.

The wind whipped through her hair, pressing it across her face, into her eyes so she couldn't see. She lifted one arm to push it back and lurched forward. Involuntary panic made her grab the windowsill and shift her weight back.

She should do it. Maybe when she saw the ground

rushing up at her, she would shift. And then she would know how to.

What was the difference between watching the ground rush up at her and watching the snowcat leap down on her?

Isabel stepped back from the window and stood staring at it for a long moment. Outside the wind howled and whistled. She held up her arm, touched the fragile skin at her wrist, and thought stone.

Her fingers still touched flesh.

She took a deep breath and sat down abruptly on the floor. It was cold, but she barely noticed. Something in her wanted to keep trying—to think of stone, over and over, to concentrate fiercely on doing what she had done so easily less than an hour ago. But she knew it would do no good. Here, in the calm of her room, she could change her hair color and her eye color and nothing else. Only when she had to could she manage anything more substantial.

And even when she had to, she couldn't shift as she was supposed to.

She sat on the floor for a long time, making a decision that shouldn't have to be made. She had one purpose: to protect Rokan. The Shifter had no pride. No stupid, stubborn pride to stand in the way of that one crucial goal.

Slowly, laboriously, she got to her feet.

Ven was back in his room. She had expected to find

him already asleep, but clearly he had chosen to investigate despite his exhaustion. The room stank of potions, and there were several new burn marks on the rush matting. Dusk had fallen while she deliberated, and the flickering tallow lamp by his bed cast an oddly sinister light. Somehow the dimness made the smell of potions stronger. He had his tunic half-off when she entered, so she stepped loudly through the doorway, and he yanked it back down and stared at her.

"Isabel?" He stepped toward her, his eyebrows drawn together. His voice was stronger than it had been earlier, but his tunic was stained with sweat, a dark triangular patch visible even in the dim light. "Is something wrong?"

She swallowed hard and blurted it out. "I can't shift."

Ven froze in mid-step. He shook his head slowly, once.

Isabel resisted the urge to avoid his eyes. "I haven't shifted once—not fully—since I got here. Since Rokan first found me." She hesitated, then said almost accusingly, "You suspected it, didn't you?"

"Yes, but I—but it—" Ven blinked rapidly. "It doesn't make sense. There must be a reason."

She rested her hand on the door, covering the gash she had left with her dagger a few days ago. "That's why I'm here."

"Something must have weakened you." Ven walked over

to his bookcase, opened the glass door, and started rifling through the volumes on the shelves. She wondered if it was an excuse not to look at her. Surely the room was too dark for human eyes to read. "Maybe your failure was so unprecedented that it changed your powers."

"Or maybe Albin has been doing something to keep them limited," Isabel said.

"I don't think that's possible. You're the *Shifter*."

She wanted to agree with him—the Shifter's powers should be beyond the reach of human sorcery. But Albin had succeeded before. Isabel let go of the door and stepped farther into the room. "It's only here that I'm limited," she said. "I could shift in my woods. I wouldn't have survived for so long otherwise."

"But there you had the power of the Mistwood to draw upon. Maybe that makes a difference." Ven pulled out one book, then another, and carried them both to the table. "I'll see if I can find something."

In books. But it wouldn't be in the books, because this had never happened before. Isabel bit her lip, wondering why she had thought Ven would be able to hand her an answer.

"Don't be afraid." He put the books down, opened one, and raised his head. This far from the lamplight, his face was hidden by shadows, but she didn't shift her sight. She wasn't sure she wanted to see his expression. "I'll figure it out."

She wished she could believe him. It was such a relief to finally tell *someone* who would try to help her. Even if she shouldn't need help. Isabel swallowed hard. "How long will it take?"

"I don't know." Of course he didn't. He didn't even know what he was searching for. "I'm supposed to be strengthening the wards around the castle, but I'm sure Rokan will excuse me from all my duties until—"

"No!" Isabel said more sharply than she had intended. "We don't tell Rokan."

Ven frowned at her, puzzled. "He's counting on your abilities. You're putting him in danger. If he knew, he might be more careful—"

"Rokan doesn't know how to be careful," Isabel snapped. Her fingers twisted in her gown; she loosened them with a deliberate effort. "It would make no difference in his behavior."

"But why don't you want him to know?"

"You really have to ask that?"

Ven's hands thudded down on the table. "You can't mean to say you're embarrassed!"

"Why can't I?" Isabel demanded. "It's embarrassing, isn't it?"

"Embarrassment is a human emotion," Ven said stiffly.

She folded her arms. "So are anger, and irritation, and fear. I feel all of those, don't I? Why is embarrassment any more human than the rest?"

"Because it serves no purpose," Ven snapped, slamming the book shut. "Those other emotions are related to your loyalty to the royal family. Your irritation with Clarisse, for example, stems from the fact that you can't figure out whether or not she's a threat to Rokan."

"The only reason for my irritation with Clarisse is *Clarisse!*"

"The Shifter is above—"

"Stop telling me what the Shifter is! I know what the Shifter is."

"Do you?" He stepped around the table, and she saw that he was angry. "Nothing I've read gives any indication that the Shifter can lose her powers. They're still there. If you can't use them, it's because some part of you doesn't want to."

Isabel opened her mouth, shut it, and clenched her jaw.

Ven's words emerged in short, curt bursts. "You want to be human. That's why you can't shift, that's why you delude yourself into feeling these things, that's why you care what Rokan will think when he finds out the truth. I don't know what happened ten years ago, but it changed you. You're not the Shifter of legend."

"Sorry to disappoint you," Isabel said.

He didn't even try to deny it. He shook his head and turned back to his books. "There are millions of humans in the world, too many for anyone to bother counting. We live and we die and we fade away, and eventually nobody remembers us or cares. But there's only one Shifter, and she lives forever. Maybe you should ask yourself if you really want to be human."

# Chapter Nine

That same night Isabel stole a horse and rode back to her forest.

It was ridiculously easy. Nobody stopped her or questioned her. One of the stableboys even saddled the horse for her. She considered stopping off in the kitchens and asking for food, but decided against it. The Shifter could fend for herself. Change into a hawk or wolf and hunt for dinner, if she had to. . . .

*The prey making that one fatal mistake. The lunge, and the crack of bone. Something warm and limp between her jaws . . .*

Or if she wanted to.

She rode out through the castle's southern gate, hooves clattering on cobblestones, and spurred the horse into a gallop as soon as she left the city behind.

It was a moonless night too dark for shadows, the stars a swirl of light against an ocean of black. The galloping was easier than before but still not comfortable; even so, she didn't slacken the pace, shifting the soreness away every half hour or so. Her horse became difficult about ten miles from the woods, and when they reached the first line of trees, he flatly refused to move on. Isabel realized that the horses Rokan had chosen for his journey to summon her must have been battle-trained; she was riding a palfrey, and no amount of kicking or urging would convince him to move forward. She slipped out of the saddle, and the horse was gone before she could so much as slap his hindquarters, his hooves raising black wraiths of dust as he ran.

She watched him go, refusing to imagine that she was still on his back, then turned resolutely and faced the trees. She understood the horse's reluctance. They seemed aloof and menacing, living creatures guarding their domain, hostile to any stranger who would dare walk between them.

But not hostile to me, Isabel thought forcefully. These woods are *mine*.

It sounded good. But the trees didn't look any different.

*There you had the power of the Mistwood to draw upon,* Ven's voice whispered in her mind. *Maybe that makes a difference.*

Maybe it did. Here in her woods, before Rokan came for

her, she had known what she was. Had known how to *be* what she was, shifting her body as easily as fog, never staying in one shape long enough to be confused by it.

*The power of the Mistwood to draw upon . . .*

Isabel swallowed hard and walked between the trees.

On the third day they came searching for her.

She was still human. She had not tried to shift; as soon as she entered the woods, the need to do so left her. She did not have to prove what she was. The forest accepted her, knew her: she was the Shifter. She would shift when there was a reason to, not before. She drank from a brook that flowed by a sunlit meadow and soaked in the mist that rolled between the trees and didn't feel the need to eat.

She knew every inch of the forest, every narrow path that twisted and wound its way beneath the silver branches, and this time her ankle wasn't hurt. This time—she admitted it, finally—she did not want to be found. She waited until the pounding hooves were so close that she could hear the twigs cracking beneath them, and then she shifted.

It was so easy, like mist swirling into a different form. She flapped her wings and rose into the treetops as the horses came thundering into the small clearing.

She should have shifted into a hawk, caught an updraft,

and soared away. They were nothing to her, the riders of the horses; even the one in the lead, with his angular jaw and determined dark eyes. She was merely curious, and that was her mistake. The sparrow perched on the lowest branch of a maple tree and watched.

The second rider pulled off her hood. Blond hair spilled over her black cloak, obscuring for a moment the fury on her face. "Well? Why are we stopping? To give her a perfect target?"

"Be quiet, Clarisse. I'm trying to listen."

"For what? You'll be dead before you hear anything."

"She's not going to try to kill us."

"That's right. She's going to succeed."

"Would you be quiet?"

"It's obviously not a good idea. I was quiet when you first came up with the whole Shifter idea, and you see what came of that."

Rokan turned and stared at her. "That was *quiet*?"

"For her it was," Will said. "Can't the two of you stop? If the Shifter *is* watching us, I'm sure she's greatly amused."

The Shifter was not amused. She was disturbed. On the other side of the clearing someone was moving closer, a slim, dark shape that cast jagged shadows on the underbrush.

There was no reason she should care. These weren't the people she was meant to protect. They had fooled her into thinking they were, even after she should have known better, but that didn't matter anymore. She didn't have to care about what happened to them.

She didn't have to care about what happened to anyone.

"Well, I'm glad someone is amused," Clarisse said. "Did I mention that I am not having fun at all?"

"I think I picked up on that," Rokan said.

"How perceptive of you."

Something glinted through the trees. The sparrow became a hawk, and the hawk's sharper eyesight saw the knife in the man's hand. He was creeping closer. The mist rose through the ferns like tiny feathers and swirled away from his movements.

"Did you hear something?" Rokan asked.

"No. I don't know what you're listening for. Mist can move without making any noise."

The man had risen into a half-crouch. He flipped the knife to hold it by its blade.

"She might not be mist."

"Right. She might be fog, or a bird, or a rat, or one of a hundred other things you wouldn't be able to hear. This is a waste of time. You won't find her unless she wants you to find her, and if she does, she'll just come back to the castle and—"

The man raised his arm to throw, and suddenly the hawk was a girl and the girl was screaming, "Watch out!"

Rokan turned—toward her, not toward the knife. Isabel half-leaped, half-fell through the air, knocking him off his horse. The knife hit her instead, blade first.

She turned into mist as it pierced her skin. The knife flew through her body and stuck, hilt quivering, in the trunk of the tree she had been watching from.

Rokan grunted as he landed on the ground with Isabel's hazy outline on top of him. Before he could even lift his head she was gone, racing through the underbrush, her paws digging into the earth and her sharp wolf's nostrils making sight all but unnecessary.

She caught the would-be assassin before he had gone thirty yards, circling around to cut him off, her ears laid back. He didn't try to get by her, but stood and stared at her, his eyes afraid but direct. The wolf became a girl, and Isabel crossed her arms.

"That was foolish," she said. "In the Shifter's forest itself? Did you think you would get away with it?"

"I've been waiting for him to come back here," the young man said. "I didn't think you would protect him."

He was tall and thin, with a scruffy, sharp-jawed face and dark blue eyes. She guessed he was about the same age as Rokan, but his gauntness made him appear older. He was trembling—not that she needed to see that, the wolf smelled his fear—but his face was expressionless, and his eyes were trained directly on her.

"Why not?" Isabel said. "I've protected him before, haven't I?"

"But you left the castle. You must know the truth now."

"I knew the truth then."

He flinched. "The Shifter is supposed to be loyal."

"I am the Shifter." That was becoming a very useful line, even if she only half-believed it herself.

"The Shifter is the protector of the royal family. *You* must be an imposter."

She dropped her arms to her side and stepped toward him. "Do you need me to turn wolf again to convince you?"

He tensed, but he didn't step back. "Would you?"

She smiled, taking another step. "No."

"No, of course not. You never would."

That stopped her in her tracks. "What do you mean?"

"Don't you know me?"

She stared at him.

"You were there when they came for us. *His* father's soldiers. You tried to protect me and my sister."

Isabel shifted her hands into hands that wouldn't shake, her expression into blankness. "Is this some sort of trick?"

"I swear it's not." He leaned forward, legs still poised to leap. "You got me out. You didn't fail. There's still a royal family for you to protect. You don't have to serve those imposters."

She should have stayed a bird. She should have stayed away. Isabel bit back a whimper and said, "I don't—"

"Please!" He swallowed hard, his eyes never leaving her face. "You know me. You saved my life."

She crouched, curling her lips in a wolflike snarl. But he didn't run. He didn't even flinch. "You have to stop them. You have to kill *him*." She had never known a word could contain such hatred. "You're the Shifter. You must know which one of us is truly meant to be king."

"Isabel?" Rokan called. The mist muffled his voice, but it didn't sound like he was far.

The would-be assassin tensed. His eyes moved from hers for the first time, to search the trees. "You can't give me to him."

Isabel looked away.

"Isabel?" Rokan shouted. Twigs crackled.

"Come with me," the stranger said urgently. "You're my Shifter."

"Isabel?"

"Go," Isabel said, almost spitting the word out.

He stepped toward her. "You—"

"No. *Go*."

For a moment he hesitated. Then, with a quick glance

back at the mist-veiled trees behind him, he dodged around her and ran.

A moment later Rokan appeared, his face smudged with dirt and dried brown leaves clinging to his hair. He took in her lone, still figure with a glance that was first relieved, then puzzled.

"Where is he?"

"He disappeared," Isabel said. "Sorcery."

Rokan swore. "Are you all right?"

She gave him a withering look. "Of course I'm all right."

"You're bleeding."

She was. There was blood streaked over her right elbow, crisscrossing its way down her arm. The knife must have hit her a moment before she turned to mist, sliced through some skin. Absently she shifted her arm, and the gash closed.

Rokan had been reaching for her arm, his eyes narrowed in concern. He stopped in mid-motion, flushed, and dropped his upraised hand. After a moment of hesitation, he said, "Did you see him?"

She knew what the hesitation meant. So he had decided not to question her disappearance, had he? *Wise move, Prince. You might not like what you hear.* "Briefly. Tall, dark hair, large eyes."

"Large eyes," Clarisse said, emerging from the trees

behind her brother. Mist swirled away from her movements. "That's a useful piece of description. I'm glad you
caught it."

Isabel didn't even bother to acknowledge her. A moment
later Will stepped up beside Clarisse and blurted, "Why
are you here?"

So much for tactfully ignoring the situation. Isabel
shrugged and said, "I had to come back here. I had been
away too long."

"I don't suppose," Clarisse said, reaching up to extract
some twigs from her hair, "that it occurred to you to let us
know where you were going?"

"No," Isabel said, "it didn't."

There was a long silence. Rokan finally came closer to
Isabel, leaves crackling under his feet. "We were worried
about you," he said.

"Worried about me," Isabel said, "or about what I was
doing?"

Rokan's brow furrowed. He held her gaze until Isabel
stepped back, feeling a need to defend herself, not quite
sure against what.

"I'm your Shifter," she said. The possessive felt strange
on her tongue; she had just heard the assassin use it, but
it had never before occurred to her. Had there ever been
competing claims on a Shifter? *No, of course not; that's*

*what the Shifter is there to prevent.* "But I am not your slave. What I do is of no concern to you."

"I was worried," Rokan said, his voice tight, "about you."

He sounded like he meant it. But she wanted him to mean it, so how would she know if he was lying? She half-turned away, shrugging one shoulder dismissively. "Why? I can't be hurt."

"You were hurt once," Rokan said almost angrily, "and you fled to your woods. Here you are again. What am I supposed to think?"

"Whatever you want," Isabel said. "But the only thing that can hurt me is something that hurts you."

He blinked at her, then took a deep breath. "All right. Are you ready to go back yet? You can ride behind me—"

"I don't need to ride," Isabel said.

Late that night the royal trio returned riding three very spooked horses. About fifty feet behind them loped a lean, gray-white wolf.

# Chapter Ten

The rain started two days later and didn't stop for a week. Relentless and rhythmic, it hammered on the stone walls and rooftops of the castle. Every time the Shifter passed a window, she saw nothing but heavy, streaking darkness, occasionally illuminated by a brief flash of lightning or punctuated by a rumble of thunder. It made her fur bristle, so she stayed away from windows.

The wolf did not like being cooped up indoors. The castle was too cold and sharp, too full of humans and noise. She was on edge, restless and snappy, and the feeling only went away when she was near her prince. Then her edge had a purpose, and her wariness an outlet.

She followed him everywhere, prowling easily and silently at his heels. The other members of the court gave her a wide berth. Isabel neither noticed nor cared—until she realized, one day as she sat at Rokan's feet in the private audience chamber, that Clarisse was afraid of her. She rose to her feet and padded over to the princess, who sat in a carefully relaxed pose on the couch, hands open and eyes half-closed. It was a remarkable performance, but wolves could smell fear.

Isabel stood for a moment in front of Clarisse. Then she snarled and leaped.

Clarisse screamed and rolled off the couch, scraping her hip over the armrest—which had to hurt—and landing in a heap on the floor, gasping and scrambling away. Her heel caught in her gown; she kicked, it ripped, and a swath of yellow cloth fluttered away from her foot. The wolf landed lightly on the couch, turned around, and sat neatly down. She panted at Clarisse, her tongue lolling out.

Will was helpless with laughter. Rokan was trying hard to keep a straight face, but snickers kept escaping. Clarisse got to her feet and glared at Isabel, her face red.

"Bitch!"

"Under the circumstances," Rokan commented in an almost steady voice, "that's really just a statement of fact, you know."

Clarisse turned her glare on him, and Rokan lost control, flopping over on the cushioned bench. Clarisse stood for a moment, breathing hard. Then she reached down, gathered up the trailing fabric from her gown, and stalked out of the room.

"That was marvelous," Rokan gasped, sitting up. There were tears in his eyes. "You deserve a reward. A steak, or— or something. Diamonds, when you turn human. None of the legends said the Shifter had a sense of humor!"

Isabel tried to smirk, discovered that wolves couldn't, and shifted. Still wearing the gray riding outfit she had put on two weeks ago, she crossed her legs and lifted her eyebrows. "Legends can be incomplete."

"So they can." Rokan laughed again, but less easily this time. He straightened and rubbed one hand on the armrest of the couch, not quite meeting her eyes. He had been more comfortable with her when she was a wolf.

Isabel had also been more comfortable with herself when she was a wolf. Then she had known what she was doing—protecting Rokan—and it hadn't mattered why. She stretched her arms and shifted back.

Except she didn't.

At first startled, then furious, she tried again and again. Nothing happened. Her legs remained legs, ridiculously weak and furless; her face felt flat and cold, her body ungainly. She drew her lips back in fury.

"Isabel?" Rokan said, distinctly uneasy now.

Humans couldn't draw their lips back; it would make them look funny. Isabel took a deep breath and pressed her lips together.

"Sorry," she said, very glad that Clarisse had already left the room. "Sometimes it takes a second for me to get used to a new shape." She sat up straight and almost fell off the couch; her balance was different without a tail. "I like being a wolf. But I think the Lady Isabel had better make an appearance at court again."

Rokan bit his lower lip and glanced sideways at Will. "Uh—that won't be necessary."

Of course it wouldn't. She had taken charge, that day when Daria disappeared, in a way no innocent noblewoman would have. And for days a wolf had been padding along at Rokan's heels.

She tried to think of a way to hide the slip and couldn't, so she ignored it instead. "How are they taking it?"

"Pretty well. I think a lot of them suspected. Many are pleased, because—" A barely discernable pause. "Because if it makes me safer, it makes the kingdom more stable."

Because it lent legitimacy to the throne. Made him seem like a real king, even though he wasn't.

*You're my Shifter.* She could still hear the intensity in that angry voice, see the sense of betrayal in those dark blue eyes. It was impossible to think he had been lying.

As a wolf, none of it had mattered. She had known she was loyal to Rokan, would have protected him with her life. That was the way it should be. She tried, one last futile time, to change back, and when nothing happened despair rose in her throat. What difference did it make whose Shifter she was, when she couldn't be the Shifter at all?

Ven's door was unlocked, but he wasn't there. Isabel hesitated in the doorway, surveying the room. Ven's scent filled the air, mingling with the dusty smell of books and the rotten tinge of potions. He had been here fairly recently. She realized that she was using a wolf's sense of smell and sighed. Then she walked over to the table, where a book lay open.

A red-haired woman stared up at her from the page, large green eyes narrowed in a sharp, triangular face. Isabel flipped a page and met the gaze of a fat old woman with curling gray hair. The face was completely unfamiliar, but the eyes. . . . She frowned and turned the book over to read the title.

*Portraits of the Shifter.*

Isabel turned another page, then another. All of these women—a few men, too—were her. They were her as much as the familiar face she had been wearing for most of the past few weeks. She didn't recognize any of them. A few

were beautiful. Most were not. They were plain, inconspicuous—the types of people you wouldn't notice, wouldn't
remember. Beauty had both its uses and its disadvantages.
The Shifter used it only when it served her purpose. Some
of the women were fat. Some were old.

They weren't women at all. They were just masks. Isabel
wondered if the old ones had felt pain in their bones, if the
men had been stronger than the women. As a wolf, she had
wanted to hunt. Her disguises always went more than skin
deep.

Isabel continued leafing through the book. The eyes
stared at her from the pages, calm and blank, revealing
nothing. Nothing of who was behind the mask.

If anyone was.

Not any*one*. Anything. Fog and mist, emotionless,
drifting . . . bound to a single purpose by a magical compulsion that forced her to take on form, to deal with . . .
life.

Maybe she was nothing but the compulsion. Maybe the
compulsion had formed even the fog.

She felt a burning at the back of her eyes. Which was
ridiculous. The Shifter didn't cry.

*Tears falling, not leaving a mark like the blood, and that
seemed wrong. . . .*

She slammed the book shut and tracked Ven's scent to

the one window in the cluttered room. When the trail kept going, she twisted around and saw the uneven stones on the outside of the tower, suddenly understanding where he was. There were spells it would be far too dangerous to practice in a small enclosed room, spells that, perhaps, he didn't want Albin to find him working on. Spells having to do with her?

Isabel glanced down once at the dizzying drop into the courtyard below, then reached for the first stone and pulled herself up.

When she vaulted over the battlements and onto the roof several seconds later, she found Ven sitting cross-legged on the flat surface of the rooftop. Next to him lay an open book, a bowl full of foul-smelling liquid, and several glass vials. His eyes widened.

"Sorry to interrupt," Isabel said.

"No. It's not—I'm glad to see you." He started to push himself off the ground, then changed his mind and merely closed the book.

Isabel turned her back on the eagerness in his eyes and leaned her arms against the slanted wall. The sun cast faint warmth on her neck and shoulders. She could see the trees on the hills to the south; when she tried, her eyesight became even sharper, and she could see every individual leaf, red or yellow or stubbornly green. The sky was white with fog that softened the edges of the hills—as if the mist from her woods was gathering force and coming for her. A bird swooped across her view, arced, and came to rest on a roof-top below.

"I saw your book," she said. *"Portraits of the Shifter."*

She couldn't see his face, but she could hear the caution in his voice. "Did you recognize any of them? Of you, I mean?"

She hadn't, but she didn't say so. "I'm not wearing the bracelet in any of the portraits."

She heard his indrawn breath and knew he was about to lie to her. She didn't turn. He would be less guarded if she couldn't see his face. "It hasn't been used for years. It was part of the original spell that bound the Shifter in the first place."

The bird took wing, wheeled once, and soared over the castle walls. Isabel watched it go. "Then why bring it out now?"

"After everything that had happened, Rokan didn't know how far you had reverted to being wild. Part of its magic was that it would keep you from harming the prince."

That *was* a lie. But so, Isabel realized suddenly, was everything she had been told about the bracelet. She lifted her arm, twisting her wrist so the white and red crystals lay flat against her skin. Pretty. She could still feel Rokan's fingers on her wrist, deftly fastening the clasp. She liked the bracelet.

"That's not why." She spoke slowly, but without any doubt. "He thought it could *re*bind the Shifter. Create an allegiance to a new king, a new dynasty."

He didn't reply. He didn't have to.

"Fool. A *bracelet*?" She ran the fingers of her other hand along the tiny crystals. True, it had helped confuse her—but only because her jumbled memory had latched onto that one familiar thing. Focusing on the bracelet now, she could feel the tendrils of power clinging to it, thrumming with magic despite the centuries it had lain dormant.

"Fool," she said again—but that wasn't right. Rokan was no fool. She turned around and noted the whiteness around Ven's lips. "Did you tell him it would work?"

Ven opened his mouth, then closed it.

A number of things were suddenly clear to Isabel. It had never made sense for Rokan to believe she wouldn't find out the truth about his father. "Did you tell him it would make me forget my previous allegiance, and what happened last time I was here? That it would make me disregard the truth even if I did discover it?"

"I thought it . . ." He faltered under her gaze. "I thought it might."

"And you wanted him to try. You wanted to see the Shifter."

He bit his lip.

Isabel shook her head. She should have been disgusted by Ven's disloyalty, by the way humans always placed their wants above their duties. Instead she was amused. Besides, by sorcerers' reckoning, Ven had done the right thing by putting his studies first.

Not that there had been anything disinterested or scholarly about it. Her amusement faded, replaced by an embarrassment that was almost guilt. Ven had gone to such lengths to seek out a legend and instead found a damaged, faded version of what she was supposed to be.

"I told him what he wanted to hear," Ven said. "He would have gone to get you no matter what I said."

There was a moment of silence while Isabel turned that over in her mind. Then Ven added, almost in a whisper, "I'm glad you're back."

Isabel realized that it hadn't even occurred to her to go tell him she was back. She hadn't thought of him at all until she was in human form again. "I'm sorry—"

"No. I'm sorry." He took a deep, shaky breath and got to his feet. "You left because of what I said. I shouldn't have said it. I compared you to a legend and got angry at you because you're not—"

"But I should be the legend." She turned back toward the battlements, so it would be easier to say what she had to say. "If something inside me wants to be human, I have to root it out and kill it. I can't protect Rokan this way."

"Nothing inside you wants to be human. You were a wolf—"

"And now I'm not. And now that I'm back in this castle, I can't shift back." In the distance mist rolled and twisted through the trees, dimming the brilliant reds and yellows of their foliage. "I think it's because there's something human about the Shifter. I think maybe . . . maybe I was human before I ever was the Shifter."

"No."

Isabel turned to face him then. He didn't want to hear this; not as much, she thought, as she didn't want to say it. Too bad for both of them. "You're the one who told me the origins of the Shifter are unknown. Maybe I'm not some ancient entity chained to the royal family. Maybe I was not found, but—created."

"Isabel—"

"And maybe what they created me *from*," Isabel finished, raising her voice, "was a human being!"

"It's not true. Trust me, I've thought of it. All these problems aren't your—"

"Of course they're my fault! I'm not what I'm supposed

to be!" She gripped the rough-hewn stone behind her. "He summoned me for his protection, and I can't be what he needs me to be. I thought it might be because *he's* not what he's supposed to be, either—so I ran, just like I ran ten years ago—but then he was in danger and I couldn't let him die. And once I had saved him, I couldn't let him go back to the castle alone. I can't help it, it's what I am—what I'm supposed to be—what I *want* to be—"

She broke off, suddenly aware of how high her voice had risen. Ven was staring at her with wide, startled eyes, and a sudden rush of embarrassment flooded through her, hot and painful. The Shifter out of control, ranting like a mad-woman . . . she doubted there was precedent for *that* in any of Ven's books.

"It's all right," Ven managed to say, though his voice sounded a bit strangled. He took a step toward her, half-lifting one hand to pat her on the shoulder. "It's all right."

Isabel pressed back against the battlements, feeling the firm stone against her shoulder blades and struggling to regain her composure. She almost took a deep breath, then remembered that she didn't have to and instead shifted her breathing steady. After a moment she forced herself to meet Ven's eyes.

"It's not all right," she said. "Rokan was wrong to come

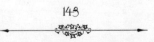

for me, wrong to trust me." She pushed upright, trying to think clearly and coldly. "What possessed him to take such a risk in the first place? Other kings in other lands survive their reigns without the aid of supernatural beings."

Ven dropped his hand back to his side, his cheekbones stained red. He was as embarrassed by her outburst as she was. "The kings of Samorna have grown used to having a bit more security."

"His father didn't have it."

"Rokan is not his father."

"*That*'s perfectly clear. But he could have managed without me. He had Clarisse, and the guards, and he thought he had Albin...." Ven's fists were clenched at his sides, the color gone from his face. Isabel narrowed her eyes at him.

He took two steps back, but she leaned forward menacingly, pinning him with a predator's glare. A fierce, sweet thrill coursed through her. She was a wolf about to go for the throat. "*Tell me.* Why was he so desperate?"

Ven drew in a quick, sharp breath. "Because of you," he said. "He needed you because he was afraid of you. Because—" He stopped, eyes darting suddenly from side to side, his jaw working silently.

"What?" Isabel snapped.

"Something's wrong." Ven backed away—from her, she thought at first; then she realized he was moving in tiny

circles, like a frantic trapped bird. "Someone just broke through my wards."

If someone was watching them with magic, she couldn't feel it; but she couldn't detect spells that didn't manifest in ways perceptible to her animal senses. Isabel's skin tingled as she reached out with every nonhuman sense she had; she closed her eyes and knew, by the way the air moved around their bodies, that she and Ven were alone. She sensed nothing.

Until, all at once, she did.

It was the wrench of something breaking. Not a ward. Something within Ven.

She snapped her eyes open in time to see Ven's widen. He gasped and flung his arms up. Rainbow colors shimmered for a moment in the air around his outstretched hands. Then they exploded into nothingness and were gone. Ven's hands closed on empty air, and he fell.

He pitched forward to his knees, his eyes still fixed on her, then fell flat on his face. Isabel leaped forward, but not in time to catch him, and he landed hard on the rough stone of the rooftop. She grabbed his shoulders, rolled him over, and lowered her head to listen for breathing. There was nothing but silence.

"Ven," she whispered, but the name died only half out of her mouth. She knew there was no one to hear her.

She was the Shifter. She knew what death looked like.

She stared for a moment at his face, at the open blue eyes and slack mouth, and something very human rose within her. She made a halfhearted attempt to block it, but the effort had no will behind it.

Two fat wet drops splattered onto Ven's shoulder, spreading tiny moist circles on the silk of his tunic. Isabel blinked, and the next few drops curved down her cheek instead of falling. She lifted her hand automatically to wipe them dry, then stared at the streaks on her fingers in horror.

Carefully she shifted her cheeks dry, and her eyes. Then she reached within herself and did the same to that treacherous, unwanted part of her that was causing her pain. By the time she rose to her feet and slowly backed away from the body, the pain was gone and buried, and her mind was working with crisp clarity. The girl who stood gazing down at Ven's body was the Shifter. Nothing else.

Isabel concentrated fiercely on what she had learned about sorcery in hundreds of years of defending the royal family. The knowledge came in a flood, interspersed with fragments of memory. Herself as a cat, watching a wizard at work . . . deflecting a spell . . . approaching a sorceress . . . coolly pushing a knife through magic wards and into flesh. At any other time the memories would have interested her most. But now she didn't need memories. She needed information.

She had to find out who had killed Ven, because . . .

Grief floated at the edge of her feelings, burrowing around the defenses she had just set up; a loneliness that would overwhelm her if she let it. For a moment she stood perfectly still, barely daring to breathe. And then the grief receded and was gone, and she breathed in once.

She had to find out who had killed Ven, because he might try to kill Rokan next.

The Shifter took one last look at the body lying on the weatherworn stone. Then she turned and walked to the edge of the rooftop, making no sound as she lowered herself down the side of the wall, her movements as tight and controlled as those of an animal on the hunt.

# Chapter Eleven

Isabel found Rokan in the stable yard preparing for a ceremonial ride through the capital city. It wasn't the ideal place for any type of conversation; he was surrounded by guards and nobles and looked distinctly unhappy. But when he saw her, his face lightened, and he gestured to a stable hand to bring another horse.

"*Thank* you," he said fervently when she had mounted and brought her horse up next to his. "Lady Zabia was going to ride next to me, and I couldn't think of a way to get out of it without starting a minor war. Which I might have been willing to risk, except I'm not sure I would win it. Try to act like we're conferring about terribly important and serious matters."

Isabel didn't match his smile. She waited until the

procession left the castle gates and started through the steep, narrow cobblestone streets, where the clatter of hooves provided cover for her words. Then she said, "Ven is dead."

Rokan turned his horse a bit too sharply, and the gelding snorted and tossed its head reproachfully. The prince took a deep breath, and Isabel saw how deliberately he relaxed his grip on the reins.

He was silent for a long moment, which she spent scanning the narrow alleys and the other members of the procession with equal vigilance. She found that she could focus separately with each eye, allowing her to survey their surroundings for danger while simultaneously watching Rokan's face. She was fairly sure she couldn't have done that two weeks ago. Her stay in the Mistwood had made her stronger.

For all the good it had done her.

"I'm sorry," Rokan said finally. It was not what she had expected him to say.

"I don't know who killed him," she said, answering the question he should have asked. They had reached the main boulevard of the city now, and people were cheering from the rooftops. "But there was magic involved."

Rokan matched his horse's pace to hers so that he could turn and watch her face. "Albin?"

"Not directly, though I'm sure he was behind it." Seeing two things at once was giving her a headache. Isabel reverted to human sight. "The spell that killed Ven couldn't be used from far away. It was someone in the castle."

Rokan shivered and pulled his cloak tighter around his shoulders. "Why would anyone want to kill Ven?"

Isabel knew the answer to that: he had been about to tell her something important. But she had no intention of letting Rokan know that she had been there, had seen a man die and been unable to stop it. "Probably," she said, "because Ven was protecting you."

Rokan nodded. He rubbed his thumb back and forth across his lower lip, then said, "But that doesn't really matter, does it? I don't need sorcerers. I have you."

The question dropped like a stone, for all that he tried to make it sound casual. He watched her as if he was trying to piece together a puzzle, waiting for . . . what?

"Of course you do," she said coldly.

The rest of the ride was silent and uncomfortable. Rokan kept glancing at her sideways, but every time he opened his mouth to speak he changed his mind. By the time they clattered back into the castle courtyard, Isabel was sure he was wishing he had ridden with Lady Zabia instead.

She spent the next few days searching every guest room in the castle, but found nothing to hint that any of the

occupants was a sorcerer. She was caught twice, despite all her efforts, but the ones who caught her—a serving maid and a cook—just turned and left her to continue with her work. Which, at least, settled the question of whether *everyone* in the castle knew she was the Shifter.

She finished the last room late at night and stood for a moment seething in frustration. She glared at the empty bed of a visiting baron who was spending the night in someone else's, trying not to think about what she had to do next.

Rokan depended on her. He would be left with nothing to rely on after she told him.

*Better he find out now than later.*

She started to turn, but she had waited too long to make the decision, and the pause had stripped away some of her certainty. The Shifter would have gone to him right away. The Shifter would have done it weeks ago. The Shifter had no pride, no need to prove who she was.

"I'm not the Shifter." She said it out loud, surprising herself, testing how it would sound when she said it to Rokan. It sounded like a lie.

She forced herself to think of Rokan dead. Even holding the image in her mind was difficult; her whole being recoiled from the thought, from a hurt so raw it was painful just to imagine it. What would it be like if Rokan, not

Ven, had fallen while she watched? All his wit and enthusiasm and dreams gone in a moment of careless inattention.
Her throat tightened until she couldn't breathe.

She knew what death looked like, felt like, smelled like.
She even knew what a dead king—

A flash of memory, almost. It didn't last long enough
for her to grasp it, but on its tail came anguish so sharp
she gasped out loud. A faint hint of what it felt like, for a
Shifter, when a king was killed.

Not again, she thought, and managed to leave the room
with almost no effort at all.

The guards let her pass, watching her but making no move
to stop her. She felt them turn to stare at her as she entered
Rokan's room and closed the door behind her.

The room was dimly lit, making the foam in the tapestry of the sea look starkly white. She shifted her eyes as she
started toward the bed. She saw that it was empty, stopped,
sniffed the air, and turned toward him. He was standing
by the window at the end of his room, his back to her, staring out into the darkness. She had not been quiet when she
closed the door, but he didn't turn.

"Your Highness," Isabel said, not sure why she was suddenly so formal. She tugged at the edges of her sleeves. "It's
Isabel."

"I know." There was an undertone of bitterness to his voice. "Who else could it be?"

A moment passed before she grasped that. It made her angry, and she took two quick steps toward him. "If I was the one you were thinking of, I would probably be coming with a knife."

"No. She wouldn't have had the courage for a knife."

Isabel stopped halfway between the door and the bed. Rokan said, in a voice so quiet she barely heard it, "I know that, yet I still miss her."

He didn't look at her, just kept staring out the window. All but one candelabra had been put out, casting his face in shadows so deep that even her cat's eyes could barely make out his features. But something about the line of his jaw, the set of his shoulders beneath the black silk tunic, stirred instant empathy in her. She wondered why. Could the Shifter ever be lonely?

The question released a flood of memory. Not of her past lives as Shifter, of the castle and the court, but of her woods. She had never thought much about the time before Rokan came to find her; she hadn't been human for most of it, and animals didn't remember the way humans did. A vague blur of images, of hunting and running and flying, had been enough. But suddenly she knew that, through it all, she had been desperately alone. And lonely.

She had spent a summer with a pack of wolves but had never really been one of them; they had known what she was. She had circled above the trees with a flock of birds, but when they headed south, she stayed behind. She had passed other deer in sunlit meadows, but they had watched her warily, sensing the wolf she had been.

And suddenly she knew why she had allowed Rokan to catch her. It hadn't been her ankle. She could have shifted her ankle whole.

The room had been silent for a long time. Rokan turned from the window. Now she could see his face, save for a wedge of darkness that arced around the side of his chin and the corner of his eye. Behind him the sky was as black as his eyes.

She shouldn't be here. She couldn't help him with his grief. She had already started toward the door when Rokan said, so quietly a human might not have heard, "Please talk to me."

She stopped in mid-turn, surprised. "About what?"

"Just—talk to me. About anything."

She searched for something to say. She couldn't come up with a single thing.

After an awkward silence, Rokan sighed. "I'm sorry. I know you're not . . ." He stopped. "Sometimes I forget what you're not. What you are." He half-smiled, a bitter, self-contemptuous smile, and turned to the window again. "I can be an idiot that way. I'm truly sorry."

Isabel stood there, not sure what to do. She could hear him breathing: slow, unnaturally even breaths that went in and out with great care.

Rokan stepped away from the window to his neatly made bed. He threw himself backward on the maroon bedspread and stared up at the canopy. "My father once said that being alone is the price of greatness. But it was easy for him to believe that. He liked being alone. My mother was lonely all her life, and she hated it."

"Didn't she die when you were very young?"

"Yes. But I remember her."

Something in his voice woke a memory in her. This was ridiculous—the Shifter didn't have parents. She was imagining it, wanting to understand her prince. Ven had been right. She wanted to be human.

She wanted to be human because Rokan was human.

"She didn't even have us." He sat up. "My father didn't want me to become weak. Feminine. He was ambitious for me, even before—" He stopped short, shook his head. "By the time Will was born, it was clear I was healthy, so Will wasn't so important to him. She was so happy then, because she had someone to take care of."

"How did she die?" Isabel asked.

"She got sick and she died. The whole thing took two weeks." A muscle twitched along Rokan's jaw. "My father gave me one day to cry. The next day I had to start fencing lessons."

Isabel walked forward soundlessly until she stood at the foot of the bed. She put both hands on the polished wooden bed rail, leaning forward so her eyes were level with his. "You hated him."

Rokan shook his head, lines of shadow cutting through his face. "I loved him. I thought he knew best. He wanted me to be strong."

"But—"

"It didn't matter. A week later I found out the truth about—" Rokan stopped short again and turned his head slightly so that his eyes were in shadow again. Isabel saw his throat convulse as he swallowed.

About how he became king. She knew what he had been going to say. She waited.

"About—" Rokan said, and stopped again.

Isabel's heart pounded. A part of her longed for him to confide in her, to rely on her for protection even from this. But he was incredibly stupid if he did. He was foolhardy for even thinking about it.

"About his mistresses," Rokan finished. "I never felt the same way about him afterward."

Isabel let go of the bed rail. "How did you find out?"

Rokan's chest heaved—with relief or regret, Isabel couldn't tell. "Clarisse told me."

"Sweet."

"She didn't realize how upset I would get. She didn't care that much." He traced a line of embroidery along the fabric of the bedspread. "I still don't know how she found out, but she was always better at seeing reality than I was. She never trusted Daria."

So the conversation had come full circle. "Does she trust anyone?"

"No. But she doesn't *dis*trust everyone, and she warned me about Daria. We had a screaming fight. I said things . . . and she was right. I should have listened to her."

"Clarisse told you not to come get me," Isabel pointed out. "You would be dead now if you had listened to her."

Rokan smiled. It was slow and peaceful, a smile she hadn't seen on his face since Daria's betrayal. "Yes, she was wrong about you. Good to know."

The silence that followed felt almost companionable except for the hot lump at the back of Isabel's throat.

Finally Rokan stirred. "I'm sorry, Isabel. I never asked what you came here to tell me."

She didn't even think about it. "Nothing in particular. I

was just—nervous. Shifter instinct." Was there such a thing? "But you seem safe."

"With you around, always."

She turned smoothly, not wanting him to see her face, and left the room without another word.

# Chapter Twelve

The guests for Rokan's coronation began arriving in full force the next day, and Isabel barely had time to breathe. Every day new dukes and commanders and princes from various outlying countries arrived, all with entourages of family and servants and hangers-on. Now she knew what all the empty rooms in the castle were for. Within five days almost all of them were full, and it was still several weeks until the actual coronation.

She didn't have much opportunity to speak to Rokan, who had to greet every new arrival personally. It was probably for the best. The weight of the secrets between them threw her off balance; being around him distracted her from protecting him.

One day, though, Rokan summoned her to the gardens.

He was sitting on a stone bench waiting for her, his elbows on his knees, and when she approached, his sudden smile made his eyes glitter in the sunlight.

Isabel sat next to him on the bench and regarded him warily. She had learned to pay attention to the variations in Rokan's smiles. There was the sideways half-smile when he found something amusing; the slow, contented smile that appeared only rarely these days; and the wide, dazzling, unrestrained smile she had so far seen only twice, when he first came for her in the Mistwood and when they watched the hawk soar against the sky. And there was this one, the reason for her watchfulness: the impish grin that meant he wanted to do something he knew was stupid and was going to do it anyhow.

"It's getting crowded in the castle, isn't it?" Rokan said, stretching his legs out in front of him. "And it will be even more crowded before long. This would be a good time to get out and go for a ride."

"Certainly," Isabel said repressively. "And a grave insult to whichever dignitaries arrive when you are not here to greet them."

"Isn't it fortunate that there are certain dignitaries I wouldn't mind insulting?" He rested his elbows on the back of the bench. "And I'd like to go riding with you again. The Duke of Elmbeg is going to be here this afternoon, and he's going to spend at least an hour talking about how many ships he has. I think I could miss that without doing any great damage to my rule."

"It's an unnecessary risk," Isabel said, remaining rigidly upright.

"I could get Clarisse to take my place. I'm sure *she* wouldn't insult anyone."

Isabel snickered despite herself, and Rokan tilted his head back with a satisfied smile. "Couldn't you at least change your shape to look like me and take my place? That must be one of the tricks the Shifter plays."

From the shiver of almost-memory that ran through her, Isabel knew he was right. "Now is not the time. Maybe after you're crowned I can spare some energy to arrange for your outings."

"Easy for you to say," Rokan said with an exaggerated sigh. "You're immortal. The days go faster for you."

No, they don't, she thought, and a flash of anger made her say, "Actually, there are a few immediate problems we need to deal with. There's a rumor that some of the northerners are going to refuse to attend your coronation. They claim there's something illegitimate about it. I don't think they would dare, but I'm going to concentrate on stopping the rumor."

Rokan tensed, and she immediately regretted it. He

replied without meeting her eyes, his face flushed. "Some of the more distant of the northern dukes are nursing a belief that I have no right to the throne. There was—uh—a hundred years ago, a contested succession—"

"It doesn't matter," Isabel cut him off. She couldn't bear to watch him stumble through such a patently ridiculous story. A hundred years ago the Shifter would have prevented contested successions. "I'll take care of it. I should mention that most of those dukes are friends with Owain, and *he* hasn't showed up yet."

"He will." Rokan grimaced. "If he stayed away, it would mean he was afraid. He wouldn't besmirch his honor like that, not even if he was convinced I would kill him upon arrival."

Which might not be a bad idea, actually. But she knew better than to suggest that to Rokan.

Duke Owain arrived two days later, accompanied by a thin, insubstantial wife and a surprisingly sparse collection of servants. He had not been seen at court since his niece and the high sorcerer had tried to kill Rokan. Isabel wanted to hate him, but the duke had a quiet dignity that made it difficult. He was staunchly old-fashioned without making any noise about it, taking no mistresses, being honestly solicitous toward the wife who had never given him an heir. He never mentioned his niece—the bastard daughter of a younger sister, according to court gossip, whom he had raised from infancy. He said something to Rokan that might or might not have been meant as an apology, and after that he stayed out of everyone's way.

It bothered Isabel that she liked him, because the thought of him made her muscles clench. Rokan still believed Owain had known nothing about Albin's plot, and Isabel almost believed it but couldn't let herself be that stupid. Owain had been a known opponent of Rokan's father, firmly of the opinion that the true rulers had been overthrown by treachery. Everyone was of that opinion, of course, because it was true; and there were people at court now who didn't know enough to try to hide it from Isabel. But the prickly northerners had always had a difficult time subjecting themselves even to a king they believed had a right to rule over them. And Duke Owain's sense of honor was pricklier than most.

With a fair amount of reluctance, Isabel decided to ask Clarisse about him.

That brought up another problem: Clarisse was very busy. The castle was suddenly full of young noblemen, all of whom either wanted to marry the new king's sister or thought it would be wise to pretend they did. Clarisse seemed to despise them all; she treated them like dogs, exhibiting interest whenever it amused her, raising hopes and then thoroughly dashing them in front of as many people as possible, making secret promises to select young men and then pretending she had no idea what they were talking about. She was especially good at finding existing rivalries and heating them to the point of conflagration. By the time the first week was over, two duels had been fought over her and three narrowly prevented.

At first Isabel worried that Clarisse had some master plan. She spent hours with wounded young men who, being new at court, didn't know who she was—and all of whom were eager to commiserate with another eligible young noblewoman. That was followed by more hours gossiping snidely with young women who were all second in line after the princess. Eventually Isabel concluded that the only motivation behind Clarisse's intrigues was sheer malice.

Her excuse for talking to Clarisse was that the princess was stoking a rivalry between the princes of Flarine and Venir, two small island states with an intense and bitter enmity that was constantly threatening to explode into battle. A war between them probably wouldn't affect Samorna directly, but it would hurt its trade, and Isabel decided to pretend that was her business. She caught Clarisse right after an afternoon banquet, fended off several approaching suitors with a wolflike glare, and pulled the princess into a quiet corner.

"What now?" Clarisse asked, shaking off Isabel's hand. She was, as always, dressed like she cared about her suitors' attentions, in a gray silk gown that managed to be elaborately ruffled and clingy at the same time.

"Sorry to interrupt your fun," Isabel said. "I don't want to keep you from making as many enemies as possible, but you're beginning to step over the line. The Prince of Flarine—"

"—is my true love." Clarisse blew a strand of hair away from her face. "Sorry, I'm impervious to reason where he's concerned."

Isabel rapidly revised her plans. She didn't have the patience to spend an hour in a conversational dance, and she doubted she had an hour before some eager young man interrupted them. "Why is Duke Owain still alive?"

Despite herself, she still felt a thrill when she managed to startle Clarisse. "I beg your pardon? I believe you were there when my brother decided to let him go. Was I supposed to kill him personally?"

"You were supposed to argue with him about it," Isabel said. "Rokan thinks Owain had nothing to do with the attempt to kill him. Do *you* think that?"

Clarisse looked at her for a moment, unblinking. Then she said, "Some men are more dangerous dead than alive."

"Including men with nieces who try to kill the prince?"

Clarisse sighed, a little too heavily. Suddenly wary, Isabel shifted her sense of smell and caught a distinct whiff of fear. "I honestly think Rokan's right about his innocence, though Owain bears part of the blame for raising Daria to hate the prince. The duke isn't the sort to want people running about assassinating rulers with magic. He'd rather find the person he wants on the throne and make them fight it out in a nice noble duel, preferably preceded by an hour of dramatic speeches."

She was dancing carefully around *why* Owain wanted Rokan off the throne, even though she was too smart to think Isabel hadn't learned the truth by now. That might be the reason for the fear.

Might be . . . Isabel turned her bracelet around on her wrist and saw Clarisse's eyes flicker toward the motion. But the scent of fear got no sharper, even though Clarisse must know that the bracelet was their only hold on Isabel's loyalty.

Isabel hid a scowl. Now that she knew how easy it was for her to manipulate everyone else, her inability to maneuver around Clarisse was even more irritating.

A slight vibration in the air behind her made her aware of several men heading over to interrupt them. "Have you spoken to the duke since he arrived?" she asked hurriedly.

That was the right question. Clarisse made eye contact over Isabel's shoulder, and three young men were there almost at once. She raised her eyebrows at Isabel with mocking regret as she was escorted away, leaving behind the scent of a faint flowery perfume and a fear so intense it was almost terror.

Straight to the source, then.

Isabel found Duke Owain in his room. She stood for a second outside his door, sniffing the odor of man and parchment and alcohol, listening to the occasional sip and whisper of pages. It would have been wiser to wait for a more natural opportunity, at a banquet or in the gardens. But she didn't want to, and she was the Shifter, which meant it probably wasn't wiser at all.

She picked the lock without making a sound—so she thought—but when she opened the door, the duke had his hands folded in front of him, no surprise at all on his thin bearded face. He was sitting at a small wooden table, a book open in front of him and a glass of white wine to its side. "Hello, Isabel."

He knew she was the Shifter, but the smell of the room remained the same. No fear. "Hello, Your Grace."

He nodded gravely. "Are you here to tell me something?"

"No," Isabel said. "I'm here so you can tell me something."

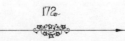

Duke Owain lifted his thick white eyebrows. "I can't tell you where he is."

Isabel had to shift her face expressionless—something she rarely had to do when she wasn't talking to Clarisse. But the duke wasn't trying to throw her off balance.

"I'm sorry," Duke Owain went on, smoothing down the book's ribbon to mark his place. "But you can understand my reluctance. You've done a good job of standing by the imposter. You almost fooled me."

The man was mad. He had just signed his own death warrant, and done it with a faint regretful smile, without so much as a tremor.

She knew who "he" was. *You don't have to serve those imposters,* he had told her, his hands shaking with fear and rage.

The confusion she had held at bay ever since Ven died welled up in her again, and she fought it down furiously. "I'm here about Clarisse," she said.

He blinked. "Clarisse?"

"I want to know what the two of you are planning."

He stared as if he had never seen her before—and suddenly Isabel realized how familiarly he had been looking at her until now. He knew her.

She reached for memories, but her mind was blank. Still, it should have been obvious. Duke Owain, loyal to

the king, would have been on good terms with his Shifter. That was why there was no fear.

Which was foolish of him. No one knew the Shifter— she was wind and fog and loyalty and nothing else. He was thinking he could rely on her the way he could rely on a human being.

*And even if I was human, he'd be a fool.* "You shouldn't trust her," Isabel said.

Owain untwined his fingers and folded them together again. "That's what you came to tell me?"

It was as good as an admission. He had been talking to Clarisse, plotting with her. "Yes."

Owain shrugged. He knew the Shifter well enough, then, not to expect her to tell him more than he needed to know. "I don't exactly trust her. But I understand her, and that makes her somewhat predictable."

Understand Clarisse? But maybe it was easy, if you were human with a full grasp of human emotions.

In her mind, she heard Rokan's dismissive voice: *He thinks in straight lines.*

But maybe, Isabel thought, he thought in straight lines because he preferred to. Not because it was the only way he could think.

It took her a moment to match her new emotion to a name: *regret.* This was a man worth admiring, if they had

met under difference circumstances. If they had been on the same side.

"Just be careful," she said, and as she turned she considered killing him. There were dozens of reasons to do it. He had as much as admitted he was harboring . . . harboring . . . her mind veered away from whom Owain was harboring, and went to whom he was plotting with.

*Finally.* Finally, something she could use to pluck that burr out of her hair. And she might need Owain, to repeat to Rokan what he had said. So she left him alive, with his wine and his books, and went to find her prince.

Rokan was, conveniently enough, also in his room. His brother was with him, and they had drawn two chairs and a small table to the foot of the bed, where they were playing some sort of game. There was a decanter of wine on the floor next to them and two half-filled goblets on the table.

She addressed herself to Will. "I have to talk to your brother."

Rokan nodded, and Will got up and left, scowling at her resentfully as he passed. Isabel took his seat and ran her finger along the flat board on the wooden table, with the assortment of colored tokens arranged on it. She didn't know how to play this game; well, why would she? "You have a problem."

"Only one?" Rokan moved one of the tokens across the board, then lifted his goblet to his lips. He was still wearing the elaborate doublet he had put on for the banquet, and he sat in a relaxed slouch; he could have been just a carefree nobleman. At any other time Isabel might have regretted cutting off one of his rare moments of enjoyment. "Want to see if you can win? He hasn't completely trapped himself yet."

She ignored that—as if it was beneath her, not as if she couldn't do it. "Your problem is Clarisse."

Rokan's face hardened. He lowered the goblet, staring at it as he turned it around in his hands. "She's staying away from the men who could be really dangerous to me. At least, she says she is."

"Anyone could be dangerous to you. There's no point—" Isabel took a deep breath. "That's not what I meant. She's doing more than flirting. She's plotting with Duke Owain."

A dash of wine sloshed suddenly over the rim of the goblet. Rokan swore and put it down, carefully but not gently, ignoring the circle of red liquid spreading across the table. "There are limits to what even you can get away with, Isabel."

She put both hands on the table and stared hard at Rokan's set face. "She's been speaking to him."

"She's probably trying to figure out what he's plotting."

176

"Did she tell you that?"

"She doesn't tell me everything. She should, but she doesn't. But she's not plotting with anyone behind my back, and if you say she is, you're a liar."

Isabel opened her mouth, then closed it.

"You just need someone to be suspicious of," Rokan said.

Isabel slid her hands off the table. "I have dozens of people to be suspicious of. Your sister has managed to get herself on the top of the list. I know you're used to relying on her completely, but—"

"But that's not all right with you, is it? Because how dare I rely on someone who isn't you."

"You're a fool," Isabel spat. If not for the ancient compulsion that bound her, she might have slapped him. "You relied on Daria, too, didn't you?"

His entire face went white. Isabel stood. "They're human, Rokan. You might love them, you might think they love you, but they have other loves and hates and fears that you know nothing about. They're weak, and you shouldn't trust them!"

Rokan shoved his chair backward so hard it fell, then stalked to the window. He spoke without facing her, his voice taut. "And you have no weaknesses? No loves and hates and fears?"

"No," Isabel said flatly.

"Really? No hatred of Clarisse to cloud your judgment?"

"No."

"No desire to run away to your woods and leave me alone? No love for a sorcerer's apprentice, that his death changes you like this?"

The conversation was getting dangerous, but Isabel was too angry to care. He would probably bring that up next. *No anger that makes you want to hurt me when you shouldn't be able to?*

"What do you mean, changes me?"

He turned around to face her, his lips white. "Do you think I'm blind? Since Ven died, it's been frightening to be around you. You've been different. More . . . intense. Single-minded. Driven."

"More like the Shifter, you mean?"

"I suppose that's one way of putting it."

"Well, you should be happy. Don't you want me to be the Shifter?"

He was suddenly silent, staring at her, his face bleak. "I am happy," he said miserably. "I need you to be the Shifter, even if I don't like you as much when you are. I know I'm in danger. It's just . . ." He drew his shoulders in tight. "I don't even feel that you like me anymore."

His eyes held something more than loneliness,

something deeper, and she pulled herself upright with a sudden sharp sense of danger. "It doesn't matter whether I like you or not. I'll protect you either way."

She was almost ashamed when he flinched. Almost. Then his face tightened, and he said flatly, "Fine. That's all I ever wanted anyhow."

She couldn't tell whether he was lying. Suddenly twice as furious, Isabel stepped around to the back of the chair. "What did you expect? You came to my woods. You put this bracelet on my wrist. You knew it wouldn't matter whether I liked you, as long as you were king. You knew I wouldn't have a choice."

"I knew. I didn't realize I would care."

"You shouldn't care."

Rokan pivoted and strode halfway across the room; when he faced her again, his body was framed by the tapestry of the sea. He spoke in a barely recognizable voice. "And if you had a choice?"

"I beg your pardon?"

He swallowed hard. "If you had a choice. Would you protect me anyhow? Or would you go back to your woods and vanish into the mist?"

Did he know those weren't her only two choices? "What difference does it make?"

"Do you know? Haven't you thought about it?"

"I don't think about things that don't matter."

His expression made Isabel so uncomfortable she had to fight not to look away. She was about to give in and glance at the floor when Rokan said, "I have to tell you something."

His tone, dead serious but laced with fear, warned her what it was. Swiftly she said, "You don't—"

"Listen to me. You want to know this." He took a deep breath and closed his eyes. "Spirits, I'm about to be stupid."

"As the Shifter," Isabel said, "I advise you against being stupid."

He let out a short, shaky laugh. "I wish you luck with that one. . . ." He opened his eyes. "My father killed the king."

*Damn.*

Isabel stood like stone. Rokan watched her, his face drained of color, his feet braced against the floor, poised to leap out of the way. Not that he could have, if she attacked.

"You were there," he drove on. "You tried to save him, but you failed. My father killed the king and his children and took the throne. And you fled."

Still Isabel said nothing. She didn't know what to say.

"I'm not the real prince," Rokan said almost desperately. "What does this mean to you?"

Isabel thought of something to say. "Nothing. I already knew."

The expression on Rokan's face would have made her laugh, if she had been in a laughing mood. "You knew?"

"Ven told me."

Rokan swore, combining several words Isabel had never heard him use before. "And he knew who you were, and what might happen. That's treason—" He stopped short, suddenly realizing what he was saying. "I guess it doesn't matter anymore."

"You thought you were keeping a secret from the Shifter," she pointed out. "Not very smart."

"Well, we've already gone over my stupidity." Rokan slumped against the tapestry on the wall. "You knew. And all this time I've been afraid. . . ."

Isabel felt dizzy with relief. She leaned both hands on the back of the chair and said, "Afraid of what? That I would kill you, for vengeance?"

The bracelet slid down her arm, and Rokan's eyes followed the motion before lifting to her face. "No. Maybe I should have been, but . . . I was just afraid that you would stop protecting me. That you would leave, or . . . or protect someone else."

That was too close to complete honesty for Isabel's comfort. She tilted the chair back and said gravely, "I have to tell you that in the beginning, I did feel a strong urge to ignore you completely and protect Clarisse."

Rokan threw his head back and laughed, and as he did Isabel felt the air tremble against her skin—the faintest tremor of movement. She whirled just in time to see the assassin swing onto the windowsill and throw the knife.

But it wasn't the knife she focused on. It was the assassin's face.

She had seen it before, in the woods, when she had let him go—but then it had been a stranger's face. Even when he had demanded that she recognize him, she hadn't. Now she did. Maybe because she was in the castle, or had been human for nearly two weeks—or maybe her mind was playing tricks on her—but suddenly she knew that he was hers. Connected to her. And for a frozen moment, as the knife hurtled toward Rokan's back, she felt no urge to stop it.

If she had been human, it would have ended right there. But she was the Shifter, and when the moment ended she was still fast enough to snatch a goblet off the table and throw it with deadly accuracy. It hit the knife and shattered, and Rokan turned just in time to take the blade in his shoulder.

He let out a short, sharp scream, then drew his own dagger with his uninjured arm. But the assassin was gone, the window framing only a cloudless swath of blue. Isabel stepped toward the window, then whirled and headed for the door.

Her first instinct was to shift into a cat, but she crushed it before she could try. She couldn't afford a failed shift now. She was confused enough as it was. She ran down the hall, up the spiral stairs, and around through an empty corridor to the bedroom right above Rokan's.

Her knowledge of the castle served her well. She knew exactly where he would come in. He would go up, because up was faster, but he wouldn't be able to go as fast as she could. He would have to be careful. He wouldn't even be climbing over the windowsill by the time she was there, waiting for him.

She was wrong. He was either brave or stupid, because by the time she ran into the room he was already there, sitting on a chair, his hands on his knees. Waiting for her.

Isabel shifted her arm to stone, hard enough to crush a man's head, and stalked toward him. There were wooden chests stacked against the wall and clothes lying haphazardly on the neatly made bed, but the room was empty except for the two of them. He sat there, watching her come. It was so insanely brave she felt proud. She stopped a few feet away.

He met her eyes. "You know now, don't you?"

She couldn't give an answer, which was for the best. No answer would do her any good. She crossed her arms, keeping them stone. His eyes were dark blue and deep set, his hair too long and tangled, and he was wearing dark clothes that had seen better days. He sat in an ornate chair, framed by elaborate green and gold brocade curtains, and he clearly belonged there.

If her stare was making him nervous, he didn't show it. He stood, and she resisted the urge to shift herself taller. "You have been misled by imposters, Shifter. I am the rightful king of Samorna, and I am here."

"I'm thrilled you could make it," Isabel said flatly.

Whatever he had expected from the Shifter, it wasn't sarcasm. His eyes flicked away from her face, then back, and he scowled. "You *should* be thrilled. Can't you feel how wrong it is to protect the one you should be fighting? I knew you once, Shifter. You loved me."

"I don't love," Isabel said, but a flash of memory told her it was a lie. She had loved him once—had loved a fierce young boy so brave it made her heart ache. But that had been years ago, and the brave young boy was older and bitter and carrying a deadly grudge.

He moved to the side of the chair, gripping its back with a callused hand. "I was a child, and I thought you loved me. You saved me for this day—so I could take my throne back."

"Indeed? Then where have you been, all this time?" She meant to stay sarcastic, but the question came out angry.

He heard the anger—she could see that—but it didn't frighten him. He ran a hand through his hair. "Nortingun. Sarswiss. Lafin. Six or seven of the most impregnable mountain fortresses. I moved every year, or more often than that if the dukes got nervous."

Six or seven—and many more probably knew. The breadth of the conspiracy took her breath away. *Oh, Rokan...*

Rokan. She spun around, concentrating on the stone wall. After a moment, she saw Rokan right through the stone, moving up the stairway in flickers of red and white, trailed by the two guards who normally stood outside of his bedchamber. She realized that she was not using vision at all; she was sensing the heat emitted by their bodies. They had reached the landing on the stairs and were hesitating, not sure which way she had gone.

She turned to the would-be assassin, her heart pounding. "How did you get to the dukes?"

"You brought me to Duke Owain's doorstep." He took two long steps backward and rested against the wall. "And then you left. You were . . . you were hurt, I think. It didn't look like you were hurt, but I think you were." He watched her closely. "You know who I am, Shifter."

And he was right. She uncrossed her arms. "Kaer."

He smiled, his triumph so blinding it almost masked his

relief. "Yes. It's all clear now, isn't it? It's time to right the imposter's wrong."

"His father's wrong," Isabel said. "Not his."

Kaer slammed his open palm against the wall. "I gave him a chance. I sent him a message, telling him to flee the realm or die."

And that was how Rokan had known he was in danger. That was why he had come to her woods: for protection from Kaer—and to keep Kaer from getting to her first. That message had brought her here. For a moment Isabel wished fiercely that Kaer had just killed Rokan and never sent it.

And of course, Rokan couldn't explain to the Shifter that she was protecting him from the very person she *should* have been guarding.

Her heart ached for him, even as she noted his progress through the walls. He was headed down the corridor in the direction of this room, the guards still behind him. The way his fingers were curled told her he was holding a knife, though her heat-vision couldn't see the weapon.

She was at the door in a flash, pushing it silently closed. She turned, putting her back to the door, listening to the footsteps draw closer. She had to shift her ears to make them out through the thick wood, which was good; it meant Rokan wouldn't hear her talking to Kaer.

"What do you plan to do now?" she said.

His head came up. Something in that movement—in the way the black hair flew back, the jaw jutted, the eyes flashed—was so familiar her heart skipped a beat. She had loved this boy long before she ever met Rokan.

She couldn't kill him. Never had been able to. Even the first time she saw him, in her woods . . . she had thought, when she let him go, that she was making a decision. But there had been no decision to make.

"You know what I plan," Kaer said. "To kill the imposter. *Prince* Rokan."

Rage flared within her. But it died just as suddenly, leaving her empty. Behind her, on the other side of the door, the footsteps paused and then kept going.

"You should be helping me." Kaer pushed himself away from the wall. "Me—not him! You're my Shifter. You have to help me win my throne back."

"I am your Shifter," Isabel said. The words were oddly easy to say.

He crossed his arms over his chest. "In the woods you saved *his* life."

He was staring at her the way Rokan sometimes had, back in the beginning. Warily. It cut more deeply, now that she understood how unnatural it was for a prince to look at his Shifter with suspicion in his eyes.

Now that Rokan no longer looked at her that way.

"Stop it," Isabel said so fiercely that Kaer blinked. She stepped toward him. "Where were you, when I needed a prince to protect? What reason did I have not to believe him?"

His jaw set. "I'm here now. And I could be sitting on my throne by now, too, if not for you."

Out in the hall the footsteps stopped, turned, and strode back the way he had come. Every muscle in Isabel's body clenched. If she opened the door now and let him see her, this whole horrible mess could end right now. He had the guards with him . . . but Kaer had her. It would be no contest.

Rokan passed the closed door and continued to the stairwell; she could hear him making his way down the stairs, back to his bedroom, to wait for her. Isabel's stone arms shifted back to flesh; she tried to fight it, but her sense of danger had passed, and her body wouldn't cooperate. She let her spindly human arms drop to her side. When she spoke, her voice was resigned.

"Don't be a fool. Stealthy assassinations are no way to convince anyone of your legitimacy. If you want your throne back, it has to be a well-staged battle—public, dramatic, and with a large number of the dukes' men in the immediate vicinity."

Kaer chewed the side of his lip, watching her, blue eyes wary. "Owain said the same thing. He thinks I should

challenge him at his coronation. Do you think that would work?"

"It has a better chance than your knife-throwing escapades."

He flushed, but his chin went up. "It will have an even better chance if *you* publicly support me. And the best way to do that, to remove all ambiguity, would be if you were the one to kill him. Will you do that for me?"

She didn't hesitate. She knew, deep in her inhuman soul, whom she belonged to and what she was going to do. Hesitation would have implied that she had a choice, and that would have been yet another lie.

"Yes," said the Shifter. "When the time is right, I will kill him for you."

# PART III

# KAER

# Chapter Thirteen

"He got away," Isabel said in disgust, striding into Rokan's bedroom.

Rokan was standing by the window, his dagger sheathed, holding a handkerchief to his shoulder. The handkerchief was soaked with blood and his face was white, but he spun around when she entered. "Are you all right?"

The question was too silly to deserve an answer. Isabel walked over to him and peeled the handkerchief away. The sharp, metallic smell of blood filled her nostrils. Rokan winced but otherwise stood perfectly still. There was a lot of blood, but no bone showing. Without remembering all the other wounds she had seen, Isabel knew this one wasn't serious, though it was probably painful. She pushed away an instinctive sympathy and stepped back.

"He disappeared before I could get close to him."

"Sorcery." Rokan swore under his breath and pressed the handkerchief back into place. The cloth was dark brown now; only the edges were still white. "Incredible. He went to all that effort to get me alone and then attacked me with the Shifter right there in my room." He smiled at her, his eyes brilliant despite the pain that bleached his face white. "He must not know who you are."

Isabel suppressed a wince. Kaer must have been waiting, not to find Rokan alone, but to find him alone with *her*. So he could force her to remember which side she was on. "You should have that wound checked," she said, heading toward the door. "I'll summon one of the healers."

"Wait," Rokan said. "You were gone for a while. You must have learned something. Tell me."

"I was trying to find him," Isabel said, glancing at him over her shoulder. "I learned nothing."

"Could you see who it was?"

"You saw as much of him as I did." Isabel was surprised by how difficult it was to continue the lie, even now that she knew how blatantly *he* had lied to *her*. She turned to face him. "Who do you think he was?"

Rokan's eyes went opaque. "One of the dukes' men, I assume. Or a hired assassin."

Not telling her the truth was the smart thing to do, but

Isabel still felt oddly hurt. "He said something before he vanished. About taking back what was his."

"My father limited the dukes' powers, and they didn't think it was within his rights. But they don't just want back what they had. They want what I have."

Smart *and* fast. Isabel decided not to push it. Sure of her loyalty though he was, Rokan was quite capable of figuring out what had happened if she dropped enough hints. "We need to make them as frightened of you as they were of your father. You're going to have to kill some people, you know."

"No," Rokan said, backing away from her, "I don't know."

"Even if I kill this assassin, they'll send another."

"Then you'll kill that one, too."

"Sounds like fun."

"Well, that's what you're here for, isn't it?"

He sounded almost angry. Isabel tilted her chin and raised her eyebrows, and Rokan lowered his eyes. "Sorry. It's just . . . sometimes I wish my father had never rebelled."

He wasn't the only one. Isabel walked over to the table and picked up a game token, turning it over in her fingers. It spun around and around, faster than any human could have turned it, so fast it was a black blur. "I would be needed anyhow. Even with a secure dynasty, a king will always have enemies."

"There wouldn't be a secure dynasty," Rokan said, watching the token spin. "The king my father killed was destroying Samorna. He wanted to form an alliance with the Raellians—never mind that the Raellians are interested in conquering an empire, not making peace treaties. He was obsessed with consolidating his hold on the northern dukes and never seemed to notice that the south was on the verge of secession. Samorna would not have survived the rest of his reign." He sighed up at the ceiling. "It doesn't matter. Nobody remembers that now. The old royal family is all dead, and so is my father, so the only person they're judging is me. But my father was right to do what he did."

Isabel nodded and put the token down exactly where she had found it. Rokan pressed down too hard on the handkerchief and winced, and she started toward him, then held herself still.

"Do you want to be king?"

He straightened. "Of course that's what I want."

"Is it?" she said. "Kings don't often get to ride alone, or marry for love. Or be free. You're the one who wants to know what it feels like to fly."

"But I *can't* fly," he said. "I'm not you. Humans can never be free."

She had to shift away a stinging in her eyes, though she didn't know why. "You could be freer than *this*."

"I could." He peeled the handkerchief off his shoulder. "But at what cost? I can't sacrifice Samorna because I want to ride and love and imagine I'm free. I can be a good king, Isabel. Especially with you at my side."

She made no response to that. She strode over to the dagger and picked it up, smelling steel and blood. "I'll find out who threw this," she said. "Have a healer bind your shoulder."

She left without waiting for his reply. Even if she hadn't known the truth, that would still have been a meaningless piece of politeness. The shoulder wound was minor, not worth her concern. She was the Shifter, and pain meant nothing to her at all.

It should have been harder than it was.

Isabel thought so every night, even though the days were hard enough. She sat in on Rokan's audiences, she attended banquets and dances, she rode by his side when he ventured into the city, and she spoke privately with him each evening about what she had learned that day. Every time he leaned forward to confide in her or gave her one of his open, trusting smiles—a tiny needle went through her, not large enough to cause real pain, just enough to make sure she was never comfortable. He trusted her, and she was going to betray him.

Once, when they were discussing the dukes, he

mentioned Daria, and bewildered abandonment flashed in his eyes. She thought, That's how he's going to think about me. And went on with the conversation.

It bothered her that she felt it, even though she had almost given up worrying about what the Shifter should or should not feel. But there was only guilt. No fear, no difficulty, no strain in keeping the secret. She didn't bother to worry about whether Rokan suspected, because she knew he didn't. She was very, very good and it was very, very easy for her.

She half-believed her own charade and didn't spend enough time thinking about it to let herself realize how ridiculous that was. She spent her time searching for assassins even though she knew where the assassin was, spying on the arriving guests even though the danger had not been invited, making sure she knew everything that was happening even though none of it was the slightest bit important. She spent hours with each duke's maids and daughters. She gathered hints and clues about what she already knew, as assiduously as she would have if she didn't know it yet.

It all went well until the night before the coronation, when Rokan tried on his new robe and practiced walking down to his throne one final time. No one was with them; Clarisse had gone to bed in a fine fury, snapping that she couldn't wait for the whole thing to be over—Oh, yes you can, Isabel thought, but without really hearing her thoughts—and Will had ripped his own robe and was having it repaired. Isabel stood on the long maroon carpet that led from the doors to the dais, watching Rokan as he sat on the throne. His head was high, the ceremonial robe falling in neat folds from his shoulders to his ankles. Even without the crown, he looked like he belonged there, like he had been born to command. Then he ruined it by slumping and staring up at the canopy stretched over his head.

"I'm afraid," he said, and Isabel raised startled eyes to his. She already knew he was afraid, but she also knew it was something he had never admitted aloud. "There's a part of me that doesn't really believe I'm going to be king."

At that moment some barrier snapped, and Isabel knew—really *knew*—that he was right. He was never going to be king. He was going to die tomorrow, and Kaer was going to be king.

Her fingernails dug into her palms. But Rokan was watching her, a fragile expression in his eyes, so she shifted her voice steady and said, "You don't have to be afraid while I'm here."

"Not of that," he said, waving off three near-successful assassination attempts as minor irritants. "I'm afraid of not being a good king. Sometimes kings make decisions and people die. I used to watch my father make those decisions

and wonder how he could seem so calm. But he really was calm. He didn't care."

"But you do." Isabel brushed a wayward strand of golden hair away from her face.

He gazed back up at the canopy. "I know. And what if because of that I can't make those decisions? Because they have to be made. I've studied history. Nice kings are weak kings, and weak kings are bad kings. What if I'm a bad king?" He got to his feet, his eyes black as marble in the dim light, fierce and intent. "Does the Shifter help the king with such matters, even when his life is not at stake? With affairs of state, and alliances, and wars?"

This conversation was laughable, if one knew what was going to happen tomorrow. Isabel didn't feel the slightest bit like laughing. And she didn't know the answer to his question. But it didn't make a difference, so . . . "Yes," she said.

Rokan's face didn't change, but his shoulders relaxed. "That will be good. That will help. You—you can be ruthless."

Yes, I can be, Isabel thought. And decided to say it aloud without the bitter tinge. "Yes. I can be."

"Good," Rokan said, and then more firmly, "Good. I'll need you, Isabel. Even after we find out who the assassin is."

"I know," Isabel said, hating herself. "I'll be there whenever you need my help."

"I'll be glad of it. That will make everything easier." He smiled at her then, a wide, brilliant, unrestrained smile. She had seen that smile twice before—in the Mistwood, when he had first come for her, and outside the city when they watched the hawk fly. It lit up his face. The urge to answer it was nearly irresistible. It *would* have been irresistible had she been human.

She pressed her mouth in a firm, straight line.

Rokan leaned forward. "You won't go back to the Mistwood, then? I'll need your help for as long as I reign." He hesitated, gathering his courage. "And . . . and I would miss you, if you left me."

*Spirits.* What she saw in his eyes now was not a command, nor a plea, but something else entirely. A hope.

Letting him believe what he wanted to believe was the best and easiest way to fool him. But Isabel couldn't do it, even if it would allow her betrayal to succeed beyond all measures.

She held up her arm, letting the bracelet slide down along her wrist, tinkling faintly.

"As long as you need me," she said, "I can't leave."

Rokan drew in his breath, held it for a moment, then let it out. In the second before he composed his face, she saw that she had hurt him; and she told herself, Best get used to it.

All at once it hurt to be near him. Isabel nodded curtly, muttered something about checking defenses, and strode out through the throne room doors. Outside, she leaned against the wall and wished more than anything that she had all her powers. If she did, she would shift into swirling mist and be gone. If she did, she would never again forget what she was.

The Shifter didn't feel guilt. Or indecision. Or . . . pain. The Shifter wouldn't have to shift the insides of her eyelids to make the prickling go away.

She spent that night trying desperately to shift, throwing herself again and again into the image of a wolf or a hawk or a cat. Over and over, until she was sweating and gasping, her failure so intense it physically hurt. She tore at her body with her fingertips, hating the flesh that kept her caged, and then shifted the bloody skin back into wholeness. And still she was trapped in a human body, a human mind that kept circling back to things the Shifter wouldn't have bothered to think about.

Tomorrow Rokan would die.

He wasn't the prince, so it didn't matter.

He trusted her.

It didn't matter.

Clarisse would be proved right.

Even that didn't matter.

After what seemed like forever, morning came, dragging frail pink clouds across the lightening sky. She stood by her window until the horizon turned blue, first pale and powdery, then a powerful strong blue that tore the morning clouds into wisps. Then she went to do what she had to do.

"I hate ceremonial clothes," Rokan said. "Have I mentioned yet that I hate ceremonial clothes?"

"You may have mentioned it once or twice," Will said, swinging his legs over the edge of Rokan's bed. "A minute."

"Well, it will be good for my image in the south. It gives me that unpretentious demeanor that merchants like in their kings." Rokan gave his robe a final tug and scowled at the mirror. "I'm counting on you to spread the rumors."

"Then you could have just said, 'Will, please spread rumors that I hate ceremonial clothes.' Everyone would be happier."

"He's being sarcastic," Rokan appealed to Isabel. "Wouldn't you say that's treason? Shouldn't you be protecting me from treason?"

"I go after the greatest danger first," Isabel said calmly. "Where's Clarisse?"

Rokan's answering grin was wistful; he had been

melancholy ever since she arrived in his bedchambers that morning. Isabel didn't smile back. She was, on the surface, preoccupied because she was worrying about his safety. The surface was well constructed. She had half-convinced herself.

Dangerous, that. But she let herself stay half-convinced, because she was used to it, and because it was less dangerous than thinking about the truth. The truth was that after today, Rokan would never grin like that again. Not at her. Not at anyone.

She watched for danger until the last second. Rokan had to walk into the throne room alone—a tradition that she remembered, or thought she remembered, had always irritated the Shifter. She stood with him until all the nobles were assembled in a thick colorful mass around the carpet that led from the doors to the throne. Duke Owain was one of the last to pass, his gaze sweeping over her without a hint of recognition.

Finally Isabel entered the throne room with Clarisse. The nobles were packed so tightly they were barely able to stay off the carpet. Isabel sniffed for fear, but all she smelled was an unpleasant mix of perfume and sweat.

"Coronations used to take place outdoors," Clarisse whispered as they walked to take their places close to the throne. It was positioned on a slightly raised dais, and the area all around the dais was empty except for twin chairs elaborately decorated in maroon and gold. The chairs were for Clarisse and Will, but they wouldn't sit at Rokan's side until after the coronation. On the throne itself, nestled in the center of the maroon cushion, sat a slim golden crown. "Much more comfortable. But about two hundred years ago, you decided it was too dangerous."

"That's because it was," Isabel said, and then they separated. Clarisse went to stand among the crowd to the left of the throne, Isabel to the right. Will was already there. He looked up at her and smiled tentatively. She started to smile back, realized how many eyes were on her, and had no choice but to finish the smile. It was out of character for the Shifter but better than publicly changing her mind.

She forced herself to work through the layers of sweat to whatever was hidden beneath the bustle of the room. There was steel here, invisible to the eye, but filling the air with its cold metallic scent. And another scent, less familiar but closer . . .

She turned her head sharply toward the man on her right. He appeared to be the Duke of Northbia, short and pudgy, but that wasn't who he was. He met her eyes for a moment, and she thought, I could still stop him. She nodded slightly in acknowledgment, watched him return the gesture, then turned and stared straight ahead. She wondered when he would move and what he would do.

A crash of music rose from behind the huge double doors, where a group of musicians were playing under guard. She had insisted on the guard. The door opened, and the music wafted in with Rokan, stiff and regal in his black and purple robe. As he passed a young noblewoman in a dark blue gown, she leaned forward slightly, and every muscle in Isabel's body tensed. But he walked past, and the noblewoman watched him go.

Isabel took a deep breath, realizing that if she had thought the noblewoman was really going to attack, she would have gone to Rokan's defense. She glanced again at the fat man next to her and hoped Kaer realized how dangerous this was. He had to be the one to attack Rokan, or she wouldn't be able to keep herself from defending the wrong prince.

There was no way to warn him, but she needn't have worried. Kaer clearly wanted to defeat Rokan himself. He moved as Rokan was about to ascend the throne—sooner than Isabel would have advised—shedding his magical disguise as he stepped forward and stretched out his hand. For a moment Isabel thought the sword in it had been thrown to him. Then she saw Albin standing next to Clarisse, where a tall blond man had been a second ago.

Rokan swore, and before anyone else could so much as do the same, there was a sword in his hand, too. Isabel

glanced at Albin, but he seemed as startled as anyone.

Kaer leaped toward the dais, and Rokan raised his sword just in time, knocking Kaer's blade to the side. The two blades met with a clash louder than the music, which was swelling triumphantly. The musicians couldn't see what was happening in the throne room.

The strength of Rokan's parry knocked Kaer's sword far to the side, but it also threw Rokan off balance; before he could regain his footing, Kaer thrust under Rokan's blade and straight at his chest. Rokan parried again, but this time Kaer held. The two blades strained against each other.

"You will not lay a finger on my crown," Kaer said, his voice carrying through the hall. The music came to an abrupt stop. "Imposter!"

It took Rokan only a moment to recover. He met Kaer's eyes and stepped back, sliding his blade along Kaer's. He lunged. Kaer parried.

Rokan took one step back, feinted twice, and then went for a killing stroke. Kaer's blade followed his with lightning speed, but when Rokan lunged at him, Kaer dodged instead of parrying. Rokan whirled barely in time to meet his counterattack.

Isabel didn't move from her place at the edge of the carpet. A dozen other noblemen stepped forward, and in a split second they were no longer noblemen but northern soldiers, with hard faces and long swords. One of those swords knocked Rokan's out of his hand, and another hissed along his neck.

The room was deadly silent. Isabel could hear hearts pounding, but her own seemed to have stopped. Rokan turned, searching for her.

"Isabel!" he cried. Ten soldiers stood between him and her, but if she had shifted into a wolf or a bear they would have meant nothing. His eyes widened, and for a moment of scathing shame she thought he knew that she couldn't. Then one of the soldiers jerked him back around, and she remembered that she was betraying him, not failing him.

Will let out a screech and flung himself into the fray; one of the soldiers plucked him off the ground like a puppy. Isabel's eyes found Clarisse, who was already watching her. The princess stood frozen, her face white, but her eyes gleamed as if she had just been handed a wonderful surprise. Then one of the soldiers grabbed her, and she struggled for a few resigned moments before giving up.

Kaer was talking, addressing the soldiers in ringing tones. She should have been watching, because he might be in danger. Instead she stared at the prince who had been in danger for months, who was staring back at her with the resigned horror of a man watching a long-feared nightmare come true. The soldier holding the sword to his neck was very still. She watched that sword, because if it so much as moved the soldier was dead.

It shouldn't have been that way. In her mind a sure little voice whispered, It will be easier when he's dead. And another voice reminded her of what she had promised: *When the time is right, I will kill him for you.*

# Chapter Fourteen

It might have been easier if they had put Rokan in the dungeon, or a prison cell; somewhere dank and dark and dangerous, far from the castle halls where she had walked and talked and laughed with him. But Isabel had advised Kaer not to trust the castle guards, and Owain believed the dungeon was riddled with secret exits. So the royal prisoners were instead held in three guest rooms, modified by Albin to make them impregnable.

It might have been easier . . . but Isabel doubted it, even as Kaer opened the door to Rokan's prison room and gestured for her to precede him. Very little could have made this easier.

The coronation had ended almost quietly, with Kaer taking the crown from his regained throne and placing

it on his head. Someone had even forced the musicians to start playing again. Nobody had tried to stop Kaer, but he had been surrounded by soldiers, and half the men in the throne room had been from the north. Danger would come later.

The room they had put Rokan in was stark and bare, no tapestries on the stone walls, no rugs on the floor. There was a bed and a chair and a fireplace. The window was gone, and there was a brick wall in its place. Albin, who was leaning against a corner with his arms crossed, had done a thorough job.

Rokan stood against the far wall, his face drawn, a line of blood across his cheek. He looked up when she entered.

Isabel met those dark hopeful eyes steadily, even when Kaer stepped up beside her and put his hand on her arm. Rokan's gaze flicked down to the touch, and it was all she could do not to jerk her arm away.

*Do you swear to serve me and mine?* he had asked her, knowing who he and his really were to her. She called up the anger deliberately and was able to keep her expression indifferent even when his throat convulsed.

"Shifter." He was going to try. Well, what other hope did he have? His voice was shaking. "I call upon your aid. By the bracelet that you wear—"

Isabel hooked one finger under the bracelet and yanked.

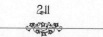

It broke, small crystals scattering over the floor, unnaturally loud in the silence.

"Did you really think you could control me with a bracelet?" she said.

Beside her, Kaer jabbed a triumphant finger at Rokan, keeping his other hand on Isabel's arm. "You can steal a throne, imposter," he said, "but you can't steal the Shifter. She's mine."

Rokan stood perfectly still. Only his eyes moved, and only a little: a quick downward glance at the scattered crystals, and then back to her face. "You knew all this time."

"That's right."

"Then why did you stay with me?"

"She was pretending," Kaer said. "It was all a trick."

"No," Rokan said, directing his words at Isabel. "It wasn't."

Kaer smiled, a smile that made Isabel move her arm away from his hand. "I'm going to confer with the high sorcerer. Watch the prisoner, Shifter."

He tossed the command off casually, but Isabel knew better. This was a power play. This was proof of where her loyalty belonged. She bowed her head in assent.

Her eyes on the floor, she heard the high sorcerer walk past, his robes sweeping crystals along the floor. She heard Kaer shut the heavy door.

She lifted her head, which felt heavy and hard to move. Rokan was looking at her. He had been looking at her all along. Not at the high sorcerer. Not at Kaer. At her.

"I am what I am," Isabel said. "And he is the true heir to the throne."

"He wants to kill me," Rokan said, his eyes black as night in his ash-pale face. "He has to, of course, but he's going to enjoy it."

"So?" Isabel laughed, a little more harshly than was necessary. "Do you think every king I've ever guarded has been a saint? I'm not a judge. I'm a protector."

"Apparently so."

She stepped toward him, and he tensed as if to meet an attack—as if, she thought, he would welcome an attack. She clenched her fists and held herself still, spitting out words. "Did you expect me to judge you, when you came to my woods? You wanted me to protect you because of who you were—who you said you were. Not because I liked you or thought you would make a great king. And you were right to expect it. That's my nature. You liked it well enough when it benefited you."

He didn't move, but there was something savage in the way he watched her. "I only knew the legend then. I didn't know you."

"I am the legend."

"No." His eyes were like spear tips. Not quite able to reach her, but not for lack of trying. "No, you're not. Legends don't laugh, or argue, or make sly remarks. Legends don't want and need and feel. Legends don't *betray*."

"You lied to me! *You* betrayed *me*! You should have known what would happen—you did know! That was the reason for the bracelet!" She broke off, astonished and frightened at how furious she sounded. At how furious she *was*. She took another step toward him, her foot sliding soundlessly between white and red crystals. "You set this up! You tried to use a cheap magic trick to switch my allegiance, to set me against the very person I should have been guarding. That's why you couldn't leave me in peace. Because the true prince was alive, and you knew the Shifter would help *him* unless you stole my loyalty first."

Rokan stepped back against the wall. She went on, advancing upon him. "You didn't come to get me because you needed my help. You came to get me because you were afraid someone else would come get me first. Well, he came."

"You knew." Rokan's fingers dug into the sides of his legs. "For how long? You told me you would advise me, you told me you would keep me safe, and all that time—"

She got her voice under control. "What did you expect, Rokan? I'm the Shifter. I do what I have to. Did you think

I'd be fooled forever? You shouldn't have depended completely on me."

Rokan smiled—an expression so unexpected that for a moment it froze her in place. "Don't worry," he said, "I didn't."

She felt the sudden surge of power, understood, and leaped forward. But by the time her feet left the ground, he was gone, leaving only the tingle of sorcery in the room with her.

"You let him go!"

"I did not," Isabel said, "let him go."

Kaer swore, long and viciously, and strode past her to the other side of the audience chamber. Above the fireplace the picture of Rokan's father was conspicuously gone, leaving a pale square of dusty wood to mark where it had been. Albin stood beneath that empty space, his face a mask of skepticism. Owain sat up straight on the ivory couch, watching her warily.

Isabel, still standing by the door, wished they weren't there. She kept thinking of them as her enemies, and it took constant effort to control an urge to attack them, hurt them, punish them for what they had done to Rokan. It was better when she could focus only on Kaer, when the force of her king's presence obscured the memory of Rokan's wounded eyes. Almost.

Kaer slammed his hand against the wall. "Of course you didn't. Men escape the Shifter every other day."

Isabel was angry; angrier than she had ever been . . . than the *Shifter* had ever been. She didn't even know who she was angry at. She took several strides into the room so that she stood in its center. From there she could watch all three men's expressions and reach any of them in less than a second. "He wants you dead. I couldn't have let him get away, even if I wanted to."

No matter how much she wanted to.

Kaer didn't meet her gaze. She could see the tension in his shoulders beneath the thin silk of his tunic. "What was that business with the bracelet?"

"Another of Rokan's tricks." Her voice sounded tired. It had hurt, a little, to break that bracelet. "A remnant of the spell used to bind me originally. They thought it might rebind me to a new king, or at least create enough of a bond that I wouldn't be able to hurt him."

He turned then, raising an eyebrow. "And it worked?"

No. She had just believed in it; the magic linked to that thin string of crystals had been nothing to the Shifter. But if it would make him feel better . . . "Partly. It helped confuse me."

It clearly did not make him feel better. Kaer gave her a long look, then said, "Fine. Are you still confused?"

She pulled back her shoulders. "No."

"Then how did he get away?"

"It was a spell," Owain said from the couch. "A good one. He and Will are both gone, and Albin can't track them. According to his sister, he purchased the spell several weeks ago."

Isabel turned so fast that her hair whipped into her face. It was brownish red; she would have to do something about that. Later. "His *sister*?"

"He left Clarisse behind," Albin said, rubbing his fingers over his short beard. "We visited her while you were ... guarding ... her brother. She has been quite cooperative."

Isabel kept her eyes on Kaer. "Why would he leave her behind?"

"He's preparing to fight," Kaer said shortly. "She would be of no use to him."

"But she can," Owain said, "be of use to you. Clarisse might come in handy if Rokan turns out to have more support among the nobility than we expected. If necessary, Kaer, you can marry her."

"What?" Isabel and Kaer spoke simultaneously. The duke waited for them to figure it out.

"Marry Clarisse." Kaer pursed his lips. "Not a bad idea. It would certainly limit his freedom to attack me, wouldn't it? And it might influence the populace as well." He pushed himself away from the wall. "What about Daria?"

While Isabel struggled to act like she had expected *that*, too, Owain shrugged again. "We're talking about political realities. The two of you have barely seen each other for years. You were only children when she decided she loved you."

Isabel took a deep breath. The floor seemed to tilt beneath her feet, as if the entire world was turning upside down. It wasn't, of course; it was finally right side up. It would just take a little time to get used to that. She caught Kaer's eyes. "I advise against this."

Kaer slanted his head back. His fingers drummed on the wall behind him. *Pit-pat-pat-pat*-pause; *pit-pat-pat-pat*-pause. The uneven lengths of the pauses annoyed Isabel. "Do you?"

"Clarisse can't be trusted."

"I can handle her," Kaer said with a scornful confidence that made Isabel wish she could watch him try. "The real question is, would it stay Rokan's hand? He left her behind, after all."

Isabel opened her mouth, then closed it. Kaer was wrong. There was no way Rokan had left his sister behind; it might have been a wise move, but it was a betrayal he was incapable of. There must have been three separate escape spells, one for each of the royal siblings. Clarisse had simply chosen not to use hers.

But Isabel didn't trust herself to discuss Rokan's charac-ter with Kaer. She said instead, "What *about* Daria?"

Kaer shrugged. "I do love her. But I'm going to be king. I don't get to make decisions based on what I want."

Exactly what she had told Rokan. So she should have been pleased. She concentrated for a moment, trying to shift her emotions as she shifted her body, until finally she *was* pleased. Kaer would be so much easier to protect than Rokan had been.

Even if Rokan was the person she was protecting him from.

"It's a bad idea," she said again. "Clarisse can't be trusted."

"Well." Kaer finally stopped drumming his fingers on the wall. "It probably won't be necessary. After all, once you find Rokan and bring him back to be executed, his influence will no longer matter."

There was something very loud about the ensuing silence. They were all watching her, three pairs of nar-rowed eyes. This was a test. A test they all knew she was going to fail.

"I won't leave you," she said. "Not while you're in danger."

Kaer pushed himself away from the wall. "I'm in danger from *him*!"

She shook her head so violently that her hair whipped into her face again. "And if he attacks you while I'm out hunting him? Or his allies do? Your safety is more important than vengeance."

"This isn't vengeance!" Kaer stepped forward, hands clenched into fists. "Do you think he'll slip into exile and leave me to the throne? I'll never be safe as long as he's alive."

Isabel's heart thudded; each separate heartbeat seemed to shake her entire body. "You'll be safe as long as I'm by your side."

"You'll pardon me if I don't take your word for it," Kaer snapped. "You haven't done a great job of protecting me so far."

"I did a fine job for the prince I *was* protecting!"

The words rang in the suddenly silent room. Isabel froze, noting the gleeful expression on Albin's face, the shock on Owain's.

The way Kaer looked at her made Isabel sure he was going to draw his sword. Instead he said, in a very quiet voice, "You didn't do as good a job when you were protecting a king."

Something deep inside her went cold. He was glaring at her with something perilously close to hatred. The king she had failed had been his father.

She tried to think of something sharp to throw back in his face. Or some way to change the subject. She could think of nothing, and then she saw the triumph in Albin's eyes.

"I didn't fail your father," she said. "I warned him, but he refused to listen."

"I don't believe you!"

"It's true," Isabel said, not sure whether it was or not. She had opened her mouth thinking she was making it up, but now it felt like a memory. "And I snatched you away anyhow. I haven't failed *you* yet. I am the only person in this castle who is completely devoted to whether you live or die. You should listen to me, as your father did not."

"Don't tell me what to do." His control was so tight she didn't realize how angry he was until he looked her in the eye. Had she been a human girl, she would have been afraid he was about to attack her. "You were supposed to keep him alive, and you didn't."

She wasn't a human girl, so what she was afraid of—like a deep chasm opening under her feet—was that he would turn his back on her, walk away, and ignore her for the rest of his life. Decide he didn't need her.

If he thought so, his son would think so, too, and his son after him, down through all the interminable years of her eternal life.

Kaer opened his mouth, but Isabel knew that whatever

he was going to say, it was something better not said. She turned before he could form the first word and strode out of the room.

The guard took in her expression and seemed glad to retreat halfway down the corridor. Isabel leaned against one of the tapestries, listening to herself breathe, not even bothering to shift her breaths steady. It wouldn't make a difference. She could shift her breaths and her muscles and her very heartbeat, but she couldn't shift away the sudden fear that underlay them all.

She had thought, once, that nothing could terrify her as much as the thought of her prince dead. Now she knew there was something worse. He could live, but choose to do it without her. He could turn his back on her and make her useless.

*What would happen to the Shifter if there was no one left for her to protect?* To escape the possibility, she had let the wrong prince take her away from her woods. She had thrown herself into this mess, so the mess had to be preferable. And now Kaer was all she had. One step away from no one. What would happen to her if that step was taken, if she really was all alone?

She didn't know what would happen to her. What would be left of her.

*Stop telling me what the Shifter is,* she had told Ven a

million years ago. *I know what the Shifter is.*

But she didn't. Maybe she had, once, and that was part of what she had forgotten in the shock of seeing her king slaughtered. Or maybe she had never known, but had never cared.

There were only two possibilities, really. She was non-human, a creature of fog and wind, created—or coerced—to guard the kings of Samorna throughout her eternal life. Or she had been human once, and something had changed her. And now was changing her back.

*No,* Isabel thought, closing her eyes. She didn't want to be human. She didn't want to have feelings, and fears, and choices. She wanted to know what was right and act without hesitation.

She released her fists finger by finger, each painful and stiff from the tightness of her grip. If only Ven were still alive. He would have figured it out by now, would have figured *her* out by now. She had told him she was afraid she was human, and he had said. . . .

Her eyes opened.

*It's not true. Trust me, I've thought of it.*

He had already considered the possibility that she was human, and investigated it. And discovered something that made him reject it.

It took her less than a minute to reach the sorcerer's tower and only a few seconds to open Ven's locked door. She hadn't been in his room since before the coronation, and she braced herself as she entered. But her memory, which so loved to surprise her with sudden visions of fear and death, was quiet.

She scanned the books in his bookcase, then opened the glass doors and moved along the shelves carefully, her nose to the spines. Before long she had a pile of seven books on the floor. The books Ven had used recently enough that his scent was still on them.

One was the book she had seen before, with the pictures of the Shifter. Two were histories of Samorna. Three were magical texts about poisons and wards and magical traps. The seventh was entitled *Tales of the First Kingdoms*.

She opened that one.

It quickly became obvious that speed-reading was not one of the Shifter's skills. In fact, she seemed to have some difficulty reading at all; apparently it wasn't something the Shifter did often. After struggling through two-and-a-half pages composed mostly of long names, she began flipping through the book, running her fingertips along the pages. Through her skin, she could feel the increased wear on the pages he had read recently, could even feel the remnants of his fingerprints.

About halfway through, she found a section he must have

read repeatedly. She put her hands on both sides of the book, squinting to make out some of the more faded letters:

> . . . And it came to be in the eighth year of his reign, that King Shapumarkin feared his enemies, for they were many and sly as serpents. And he suspected that his servants, untrustworthy Gelfolk, were in their employ, so that even within the walls of his own keep he could not feel safe. Dark heaviness settled over his heart, for nothing is so galling to a man, be he king or commoner. Then his oldest retainer told him of a creature, strange and rare, living only in a magical woods, a creature of wind and mist and great power. This creature, it was said, was immortal and powerful, and lacked but one thing: a purpose. And therefore one who gained its loyalty and gave it that purpose need never fear neither man nor beast. . . .

Isabel dropped the book.

In a split second, a thousand years passed through her mind. Wind and mist and great power. That was the Shifter, in a phrase. She could shift, of course, but there had been no reason to. No reason to do anything but be. No reason to do even that, except there was no reason to stop, either.

Boredom, purposelessness . . . those were human terms. She had felt none of them. What she had felt was so far from human that by now even she barely grasped it. She had *been* the mist that filled her woods, drifting between the trees as the centuries slipped past . . . except she hadn't known there were centuries, or years, or seasons. Even time itself, as an endless unbroken thing, had barely existed.

And then the king had come.

There had been spells, and chants, and enormous power. Sacrifices, she thought . . . but she didn't remember how the spell had worked. What she remembered was his need, his desperation. His attempt to trap her, fueled by all the magic he had gathered, had hardly brushed the edge of her consciousness. But it had been enough.

Trapped? He might have thought so. She might have let him think so. But it hadn't been his power that had made her take form, that night so many centuries ago, and follow him out of her woods.

She shivered. Those thousands of years, that inhuman need, slipped out of her thoughts almost instantly . . . too vast for the small, human thing she had somehow become. One thought remained.

*I chose. If I chose to protect him, I can choose not to.*

And what? Return to her woods, to what she had been before? She couldn't. He might not have trapped her, but

she had trapped herself. Centuries of serving her purpose, of focusing on it day after day, letting it become more and more ingrained in her, more and more what she was instead of what she did. The Shifter was now one who protected the king, and if she wasn't that, she was nothing.

She rose to her feet and drifted soundlessly from the room, not bothering to close the book.

She would show Kaer that he needed her, that he could trust her. She would deliver Rokan to him. And then he would believe she was everything the Shifter should be. Then she would *be* everything the Shifter should be, and nothing human would ever confuse her again.

# Chapter Fifteen

The throne was uncomfortable. It shouldn't have been—it should have fit him like he was born to it, like the throne in his dreams. But it was hard, and the back was not hollowed at all, and his spine kept jutting into the intricate royal sigil carved into the thick wood. Kaer ignored all that. Owain had advised him against holding a Challenge Hour, especially after he had already crowned himself a few days ago, but the duke hadn't mentioned the uncomfortable throne.

Once, years ago—when he had still been a boy practicing with a wooden sword, when he had thought he would one day face the usurper himself—he had confessed to Owain that he was afraid. Owain had put his hand over his, closed both their hands around the sword hilt, and said, "When the time comes you won't be."

Owain had been right. He had been right about so many things.

Kaer angled himself away from the back of the throne. *I'm really here. This has finally happened.* A part of him still didn't believe it, and that made it even better. He surveyed his throne room, seeking out the Shifter first.

But before he could locate Isabel, a stir near the entrance caught his attention. The nobles near the door drew away and stared, fluttering like a flock of startled pigeons as Clarisse walked into the throne room.

She did so with a great deal of skirt swishing and nodding, making it seem like everyone in the throne room had been waiting for her arrival. Her gown was an elaborate concoction of yellow silk, her hair twisted and held so that it fell over her bare shoulders just so. She dropped a curtsy to Kaer—holding it long enough that everyone would notice, but not so long that it seemed anything other than routine—and lifted her eyebrows at him with a small, confidential smile.

Kaer turned away to hide how amused he was and almost jumped when he found himself face-to-face with the Shifter. Isabel had approached the throne so soundlessly he hadn't heard her and now was glowering at him so fiercely that for a moment he found it hard to breathe.

"What," the Shifter said in a voice that didn't sound human at all, "is she doing here?"

Kaer drew himself up. He wasn't going to show fear of anything, he reminded himself, not anymore. Not even of her. The Shifter watched him with unnaturally green eyes, dangerous and predatory even in her demure powder-blue gown.

She still seemed familiar to him, which was ridiculous—the form she bore now had no connection to the ones he had seen as a child. But the day before, in the audience chamber, her hair had faded from gold to reddish brown, and the nagging familiarity of her face had stirred a memory that made him want badly to love her again. To be a naive young boy, dreaming of the magical creature who would always keep him safe, if he could only find her.

He propped his elbow on the arm of the throne and frowned at her. "I can't very well keep her locked up in her room if I may end up marrying her, can I?"

She leaned back to get a better view of his face—at an angle that should have been impossible without falling over, but she seemed not to notice. "Where is Daria?"

"She's being fitted for a gown for next week's banquet." Kaer waved a hand. "I saw a beautiful swath of silk I couldn't resist buying for her."

"So that she would have to spend all week with

the seamstress?" Isabel's eyes narrowed. "Clever."

"Thank you," Kaer said. Clarisse was now talking to a noblewoman in a green gown with ridiculously wide sleeves. Clarisse looked up at them, met Kaer's eyes, and winked. Then she murmured something to the noblewoman, and the two of them headed toward the throne.

Kaer stiffened, and one of the carvings on the back of the throne jabbed sharply into his back. This was not part of the plan. He reached behind him to rub his new ache.

"That's Lady Amri," Isabel said without turning her head. "She's the wife of the richest banker in Risan."

Risan was a southern duchy on the coast; Rokan's father had ruthlessly curtailed its trading privileges in favor of Gionvar, a rival duchy with a river harbor. The Duke of Risan had promised soldiers and money to Owain and had delivered the money but not the soldiers. Kaer wondered how much of that Isabel knew. Most of it, he hoped, if she was worth her own myth, and he would tell her the rest later. For now he merely nodded, pressing his feet firmly against the dais to keep himself still.

"My lady," he said with careful courtesy as the two women drew close to the throne. Lady Amri swept into a low curtsy, her wide sleeves sweeping the floor.

"Your Highness," Lady Amri said, rising and clasping her hands together. "I wanted to thank you for your gracious hospitality. This is my first visit to the capital, and truly, the reports I've heard are not overexaggerated. The splendor of the castle, the tranquility of the climate, the beauty of the women . . ." Here she bowed slightly to Isabel. Isabel inclined her head politely. Clarisse snorted.

"Thank you," Kaer said. He waited for her to get to the point.

He didn't have to wait long. "I must admit, there was but one disappointment. The banquet last night was marvelous, the music, the dancing, the furnishing. But I found the food a bit bland."

Ah. "I'm sorry to hear that," Kaer said. "I must have someone speak to the head cook."

"It may not be the poor man's fault," Lady Amri said. "I understand that the price of spices has nearly tripled in the past couple of years. The Gionvarian ships have not been faring well of late, have they?"

They had not been faring well because they had been attacked by Risanian-subsidized pirates, but that was none of his concern. "They have been quite unfortunate, it is true."

The Shifter was gazing at the crowd, unconcerned by the spice trade. Kaer kept his face impassive as Lady Amri put a slippered foot on the dais and lifted one arm. There were three small brown nuts in her upturned palm. "We have fared better. This is nutmeg, the most expensive and hard-to-obtain spice in the known world. We offer you some as a gift. Ground into powder, these are worth—"

The Shifter moved in an explosion of coiled muscle and blue silk, leaping over the throne. A moment later Kaer saw a red and brown head flick out from Lady Amri's sleeve, so fast it was no more than a blur. The Shifter knocked his hand out of the way, bending his fingers back, and the fangs sank into the back of her hand instead of into his palm.

For a split second the world froze. Kaer focused on the snake's head, mottled and shiny, its flat round eyes gleaming. He could see the tops of its fangs, thin and white, sunk deep into the Shifter's slim hand. Then, just as fast, the snake hissed and drew back into the woman's sleeve.

Lady Amri stared at Isabel for a second before turning, but by then two guards were already there. Elsewhere in the throne room people were gasping and crying out; they hadn't seen the snake, but they saw the guards with their swords drawn on the Risanian banker's wife.

Kaer started to rise, but Isabel hissed, "Sit," and he sat. Her hand was swelling up; already it was almost twice its normal size. Her face was twisted in pain, and he felt a surge of terror and guilt. "Are you all right?"

"I have to . . ." She closed her eyes and clenched her jaw. After a few seconds she opened her eyes. Her face was calm again.

"Why did you let it bite you?" Clarisse asked in a tone of mild curiosity.

"Why not?" The Shifter lifted her hand, revealing smooth unblemished skin and tapered fingers.

Clarisse carefully arranged a curl over her forehead, remarkably unperturbed for having witnessed an up-close assassination attempt. "If you sensed the snake—"

"I didn't sense it." Isabel turned her head sharply, scanning the crowd. "I didn't sense it because it wasn't there until the moment before it attacked. Summon Albin—"

But it was too late. The assassin smiled in mocking acknowledgment and lifted her chin. Her face blurred, cheekbones sharpening, chin narrowing. Kaer didn't recognize the woman who stood before them and, judging from her blank expression, neither did the Shifter.

"Don't bother," the woman said. "I'm more powerful than your high sorcerer."

Isabel stepped toward her, and even the guards flinched. "Did Rokan send you?"

The woman moved her head away from the sword; the nearer guard inched closer, keeping the edge of the blade against her neck. "I don't think I'll tell you."

"I think you will," Isabel said. Not menacingly, just stating a fact.

The woman smirked and vanished.

The guard swore, sliding his sword through the empty air where the woman's neck had been. Several noblewomen screamed. Kaer sat perfectly still, and Isabel lifted her shoulders ever so slightly.

"Not exactly unexpected," she said resignedly.

He wondered if she meant the assassination attempt or the disappearing act. "No. Do you think she left the castle?"

"If the spell was powerful enough. It probably was, but . . ." The Shifter took a step back and gestured at the guards. "You saw her true face, and what she was wearing. I want you to comb the castle searching for her."

The two guards obeyed her without question, even though it meant leaving their posts. Kaer watched them stride toward the doors.

"You can't leave during the Challenge Hour," the Shifter said in a low voice. "The guards will do whatever can be done."

"I know that." Some of his irritation over the guards' behavior spilled into his voice. "But chasing her isn't really *doing* anything, is it? We have to get rid of the one who sent her. Can I trust you to chase *him*?"

An expression flitted briefly across her fierce face—he would have called it hurt, if that wasn't so ridiculous. It was close enough to make a small, mean sense of satisfaction

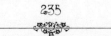

well up in his chest. She had hurt *him*, after all.

And she had let a snake sink its fangs into her hand for him. Kaer opened his mouth to say something else—something grateful—but it was too late. The Shifter had already turned her back on him and was gliding into the crowd, moving with a predator's grace that had everyone in the room drawing away.

Only then did Kaer turn to the other pair of green eyes that had been watching him all along. Clarisse inclined her head, a faint smile playing about her full lips.

It felt like a challenge. Kaer drew his knuckles across the arm of the throne and said softly, "You should be a little more afraid. You led that assassin straight to my throne. Did you know what she was?"

"How could I possibly know if the Shifter did not?"

"The Shifter saved me. You just stood there."

Clarisse lifted one shoulder. "*I* am not bound by an ancient spell to protect your life with my own. Though I am aware that, given my current circumstances, things would go ill for me should you die."

"You owe the Shifter a debt, then."

She blew a tendril of hair out of her face. "Actually, Your Highness, I owe *you* a debt. It's always a pleasure to watch that arrogant creature make a mistake."

Kaer pressed his fingers down on the arms of his throne,

so hard they went white. "You think it was a mistake that she saved me?"

"I think it was a mistake that she thought she had to save you."

Kaer jerked back without thinking, earning himself another bruise. Her smile compressed into a smirk.

"I saw the way you were watching 'Lady Risan,'" she said. "I guessed."

Kaer swore. "Isabel didn't."

"Oh, I would never claim to be more perceptive than the Shifter." The smirk disappeared, banished by a winsome head tilt. "But she didn't know what to expect. I knew you were going to arrange a test for her. It's the smart thing to do. It's what I advised Rokan to do, back when he first summoned her here."

Kaer regarded Clarisse narrowly, evaluating her through new eyes. She fingered the necklace at her throat, watching him back.

"Of course," she said just before the silence grew strained, "it wasn't a very good test. She saved Rokan, too, once upon a time. Before she turned on him."

Kaer suppressed a flinch. "She turned on him because she discovered the truth."

"And the truth is all that matters to the Shifter. So they say." Clarisse hesitated a beat before continuing. "I never doubted that she would discover the truth, eventually. But I thought it might *not* matter. She didn't act like the Shifter around my brother—not all the time. She cared about him."

"She thought he was the prince."

"About *him*," Clarisse said impatiently. "I didn't think she would actually allow him to die." She blew out a short breath. "But it never hurts to be careful, which was why I advised my brother to be prepared. Just in case I was wrong."

Kaer almost laughed. "And now you're bragging to me about how you helped the imposter escape? Do you really think that's a good idea?"

"I'm telling you," Clarisse said, "that my brother had those escape spells ready for one reason. Because even though he didn't believe me, he listened to me."

A faint quiver ran through that last sentence. Kaer didn't think it was faked. This was her one chance, her last possible play for power. A final attempt to make herself indispensable, or at least useful.

She was the usurper's daughter. He made his tone cruelly scornful. "You expect me to confer with you when I have the Shifter by my side?"

"I'm sure she wouldn't like it. How many times has she warned you against me already?"

"An understandable caution."

"You would think so." Clarisse lifted one finger to her chin. "But she didn't like it when Rokan conferred with me, either."

Kaer shrugged and motioned to Owain, who had been watching them from the other side of the room. As the duke started toward them, Kaer said, "Interesting proposition. I'll be sure to give it some thought."

His voice dripped with sarcasm. But he knew, even as Clarisse backed away from the throne, that he was going to take her up on it. And he was sure that she knew it, too.

Isabel woke up the next morning with her blanket tangled around her legs and the sun streaming in through the windows. For the first time that she could remember, she was not instantly awake. Sleep clouded her mind, and for a moment, staring at the green walls and tall windows that were now her life, she gave in to its pull. She wanted to sink back into that darkness and dream of nothing.

She closed her eyes, but there wasn't nothing. There was Kaer, the thought of him, and instant concern. She shifted the fatigue from her body and went to her wardrobe.

It was early enough that there were only guards in the dim halls—northern men who watched her with surly fear and made no move to intercept her. She paused only once, outside the prince's bedroom, steeling herself to see Kaer where she had spent so much time with Rokan. But Kaer's bed was empty.

*Daria*, she thought, and stopped in her tracks.

But he wasn't with Daria. She tracked him up a rarely used staircase to a doorway that opened onto the roof—a different section of rooftop from the one where Ven had died, lower than the towers and surrounded on three sides by curving stone walls set with iron-grated windows. Straight ahead of her, through crumbling crenellations, she could see mountains retreating toward the horizon in green waves.

She didn't see Kaer, but she could hear both him and his companion. They were sitting on the other side of tower, talking in low voices.

Isabel's muscles were so tight they ached. Even from this distance Clarisse's scent grated on her, like sandpaper against stone. Clarisse and Kaer were on this rooftop for one reason: so no one would find them. And it had almost worked. She got down on her hands and knees to sniff the rough stone, but realized when she touched the floor that she didn't have to; if she concentrated, her fingers picked up the traces of their passing, a sense that was like scent but passed straight through the pores of her skin. She swept her fingertips slowly over the stone. No one else had come this way recently—not Daria or Owain or Albin.

*You arrogant fool*, she thought, and strode around the tower.

She got a slight, mean pleasure from Kaer's guilty start, the surprise he tried to wipe off his face. He was lounging on the battlements, heedless of the drop behind him—a carelessness that annoyed her to no end—holding a glass goblet filled with red wine. Clarisse sat on the ground with her skirts spread out about her, ridiculously out of place in a gray gown that was more lace than silk. With deliberate slowness, she rearranged her sleeves, leaned back against her arms, and lowered her lashes.

Isabel strode over to her king and knocked the goblet out of his hand. That wasn't necessary—she could easily have taken it—but it was much more satisfying to see the shock on his face as wine arced in a spray across the rooftop. An instant later she changed her mind and dove low to catch the goblet before it hit the stone and shattered.

"What do you think you're doing?" Kaer demanded.

There was still wine in the goblet. Its heady scent mixed with the faint tinge of fear from Clarisse—the fear that had made Isabel change her mind about letting the goblet shatter.

Clarisse was more beautiful today than in all the time Isabel had known her. There was fake color on her cheeks and around her eyes—expertly done, but Isabel could smell the chalk on her skin. She was still posing, head cocked slightly to one side so that her wealth of hair tumbled over a bared shoulder, glimmering like gold in the dawn light. But that was for Kaer. There was no hint of coyness in her eyes when she looked at Isabel. "You don't approve of our choice of wine?"

Kaer choked on a laugh. Isabel looked at the clay wine jug on the floor near Kaer's feet and at the empty goblet next to Clarisse, its rim stained pink.

"You needn't worry," Clarisse went on, a bite in her voice. Kaer's laugh had given her confidence. "Your king isn't as stupid as you seem to think he is. He hasn't let me near the wine, or his goblet."

There was still fear in the air, but not quite enough of it. Isabel lifted the goblet to her lips, shifted her tongue, and took a sip. She tasted every detail of the wine—that it had been stored in oak barrels, that some of the grapes had not been fully ripe when pressed—but could identify no poison.

Clarisse stood, her skirt falling in folds around her legs. "Do you want me to drink it?"

It might have been a bluff. And if it wasn't, what was the harm? But Isabel folded her arms across her chest and matched the disdain in Clarisse's voice. "No. I want you to leave."

Clarisse looked at Kaer. After a barely perceptible

pause, he nodded. Clarisse inclined her head gracefully and swept past Isabel, who had to hold herself still to keep from . . . she didn't know what she might do. But it probably wouldn't be wise.

As the sound of Clarisse's footsteps faded away, Isabel faced her king.

Kaer spoke first. "She's right, you know. I'm not as stupid as you think I am."

"And not as smart as you think you are," Isabel said before she could stop herself. "Clarisse is dangerous. How do you expect me to protect you if you make decisions without—"

"She's not dangerous," Kaer said.

"I beg your pardon?"

"She's been on our side for a long time. Longer than *you* have." He swung his legs up onto the battlements, turning to sit sideways. "She approached Owain days before her brother's coronation, to discuss our plans and how she could help."

Isabel remembered the terror in Clarisse's eyes when Isabel asked her about Owain, and for a moment she wondered if Kaer was right. Had Clarisse intended to betray Rokan all along?

No. She shook her head. "She fooled Owain, then. She wasn't trying to join you. She was trying to find out your

plans. She was trying to find proof that *I* was part of your conspiracy, so she could prove to her brother that I wasn't trustworthy."

"I hardly think that's likely. And even if it's true, her plan failed, didn't it? She poses no threat to me now."

"You underestimate her. How can you trust someone who would betray her own brother? She's ruthless and—"

"Ruthless and powerless. Without the dukes' help, even I could have done nothing to regain my throne."

"You're not as smart as she is."

Kaer's lips tightened, and tension rippled through his muscles. Every one of Isabel's defensive instincts snapped into alertness, but before she could move, Kaer relaxed against the battlement, his eyes cool again. "I disagree," he said in a perfectly steady voice. "And I'm curious to know why she bothers you so much."

It was a moment before Isabel could focus on what he was saying, rather than on the tension still strumming through him, and even then she didn't know what to say. She knew why Clarisse bothered her so much. Clarisse's presence meant that Rokan wasn't completely gone. He would come back for his sister—he would never believe she had betrayed him. And because of that, Isabel couldn't shut him out of her mind. She *had* to think about him, to prepare for his attack. It was dangerous. Even now, standing

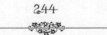

in front of her king, Isabel felt a dizzying sense of disorientation when she met Kaer's blue eyes instead of Rokan's brown ones.

"She bothers me," she said finally, "because she's a danger to you."

Kaer hugged his knees to his chest, staring out at the pine-covered mountains. She wished he would get down from the battlements. "Her brother is the bigger danger," he said softly. "Yet you're doing nothing to get rid of him."

"I told you—"

"I know what you told me. It even makes sense." He shrugged. "I suppose I expected the Shifter to do better."

Isabel had no reply to that. A sudden gust of wind blew past them, ruffling Kaer's cloak and lifting the blond strands of her hair. She imagined she felt mist against her skin, though the breeze was clear.

"I want to trust you, Isabel." He spoke with his eyes still trained on the horizon. "It's what I've always wanted. When I heard you were at the imposter's court, I waited weeks for you to realize your mistake and ride back to the Mistwood. I knew that if I could get you alone, you would remember whose side you were supposed to be on. I never stopped believing in you."

"Then don't stop now," she said. "I am on your side. That's why I'm here."

Kaer made no reply. He turned and gazed at her wistfully, wanting something he thought she couldn't give. Rokan had looked at her like that, too, toward the end. She hadn't been able to give him what he wanted, either.

The stone beneath Isabel's feet felt too thin to support her weight. She thought of half a dozen things to say, discarded them all. Kaer was right. The weeks she had spent protecting Rokan had been a fleeting mistake in the long life of the Shifter, an embarrassing deviation from centuries of loyalty. She would not fall short again. She would regain her ability to shift, she would get out of this skin with its memories of failure and confusion, and she would continue to protect the rightful rulers of Samorna. Long after Kaer was dead, long after Rokan was dead . . .

*That* thought hurt, a pain so sharp and sudden she had no defenses against it. For a crazy moment she wished Rokan was here, that she could tell him how to stay ahead of Kaer. How to stay alive. That she could explain . . .

Explain what? That she wished she could betray him without caring? That he had been mistaken to think of her as anything but a weapon?

Isabel walked across the rooftop toward Kaer, waiting until the last moment before veering slightly away to hop onto the battlements right next to him. She looked down at the courtyard far below, then stepped off the edge.

Air and stone whistled past her as she fell. She thought of wings, of mist, of fog that could be lifted on the wind and scattered through the trees. She fell, heavy and solid, trapped in a body that couldn't fly or float or disappear.

She twisted at the last moment, grabbed the edge of the windowsill she had known would be there, and pulled herself through the window with hands and arms that were inhumanly strong. When she landed safely in a pages' dining chamber, fortunately empty at this hour, she was gasping.

Once she had thought that if she saw the ground rushing toward her, she might grow wings to carry her away. Well, she knew the truth of that now.

And what difference did it make? Even if she grew wings, they wouldn't carry her away. Nothing would carry her away. She was here, and she shouldn't want to leave. Not anymore, now that she was protecting the right person.

She was exactly where she was supposed to be, doing what she was supposed to do. And that was all that mattered.

# Chapter Sixteen

Blood everywhere.

The girl was screaming, screaming. The boy was choking and sobbing. The room was filled with the scent of panic and failure, and the soldiers were closing in.

She could see the royal children—the boy, his eyes wide with terror but his chin fiercely determined; the girl with her wispy hair and eyes squeezed shut, clutching a scrap of blanket as she screamed. It was the middle of the day; light was flowing through the high windows, softened by spiderwebs thick as cloth. There was no blood in the room, but its dark, metallic scent clung to her. Failure, thicker than blood, choked her. She felt close to madness, and in that moment she knew why the Shifter had never simply ceased to exist. She didn't know how to.

But the king's children. They were her charges, too. And here they were in this room and there was no way out, no way out, and she was about to fail again. . . .

Suddenly she saw herself from the outside: a vaguely human form, shifting faster than thought, now a cat, now a wolf, now a hawk. The changes happened so fast they weren't completed at all: a half-girl/half-cat became a half-cat/half-eagle, which kept its feathers as it turned into a deer and only lost them when the deer's head became a wolf's.

She knew she was dreaming, was even somehow aware of the blanket twisted between her legs, of the way she was tossing in her sleep, but the thought of waking up did not occur to her. She was trapped. *Trapped*—she who could turn into fog and drift out through the cracks under the door. But the screaming held her. She couldn't leave.

Isabel bolted upright, barely breathing, and stared wildly around the room. It was too small, and her door was closed. For a moment she heard the soldiers pounding on it, battering it down, and felt the pain in her side where she had wrenched the arrow out.

She shivered and twisted her hand in a fold of the blanket. She knew now why she had fled to her woods, why she had never intended to come back. She could not be trapped like that again. No matter how small the chances were, it wasn't worth the risk.

And the chances weren't so small anymore. She couldn't turn into fog. She couldn't turn into anything. She could be caged as easily as a human being.

She left her room and made her way through the halls, down a side corridor, to a corner door most courtiers barely noticed. It led down to the cellars of the castle, the only area she hadn't yet explored. She knew what lay down there—the wine cellar, the laundry room, and storage areas—places not likely to be of interest. But with the screams from the dream still echoing in her mind, she yanked the door open.

A dizzying spiral of wooden stairs wound its way downward, curving around a narrow pillar of close-set bricks. A window cut high in the wall let the faintest tinge of moonlight flow down a narrow passageway in the stone, light a human wouldn't have noticed. It took her a few moments to adjust—long enough for panic to surge through her—but then her cat's eyes caught that light and drank it in. She gasped with relief but still didn't want to put her foot on the next step. She snorted. The Shifter, afraid of the dark?

At the bottom of the stairs the air was dank and chill, and it sat heavily on her skin. There were more windows set high up, but underbrush had grown over many of them, leaving narrow stone corridors that were completely black even to her.

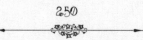

She turned right into a room where rows of vast dark barrels lay on their sides. The wine cellar. Beyond that was the laundry. Isabel hesitated at that door, knowing there was no exit at the other end. The dank air weighed down her lungs, and she wondered why they didn't shift in response.

The windows in the laundry were clear of foliage, making the room bright as day to her. It was long and narrow, nearly bare but for the white pillars supporting the low roof. She paced across the stone floor and peered up at a window opening. Each window was formed of two arced rectangles, with iron bars laid across them; but even without the bars, the window was too small to fit a child through. . . .

Her heart pounded. She whirled, fully expecting an attack, but the room was empty. The chill seeped into her bones. She tried to shift it away, but she was having a hard time concentrating. There was a thin sheen of cold sweat on her forehead, and her muscles were clenched so tightly they ached.

*This is where it happened.*

A brilliant deduction. No wonder the Shifter was famed for her wisdom.

A sudden jumble of memories welled up in her mind. A child screaming. Outside, a steady series of thuds as the soldiers battered down the door. Now there was color, now there wasn't; now there was depth, now the room was flat; now she saw the room as a whole, now in a shimmering mosaic of dozens of identical images. In many shapes, she could smell more strongly than she could see, and the strongest scent in the room was panic. And the strongest panic was her own.

There was nothing she could do. She *would* have given her life to save them that day—would have ended centuries of existence for the sake of the two squalling children trapped in that room.

But she had no life to give.

Intense as the flood of memory was, it lasted for less than a second. Isabel caught her breath and turned to go, and that was when she became aware that she was no longer alone.

"Trying to figure out how you failed?" a voice sneered behind her. "To make sure it won't happen again?"

The dagger was out of her sleeve before he had finished talking, flying across the room in the direction of the voice. She knew exactly where his throat would be, and her aim was unerring. But instead of steel sliding through flesh, she heard a muted pop; and when Albin stepped away from the wall, his fleshy throat was unmarked.

Isabel coiled like a spring. I should kill him, she thought. If I can.

Of course she could. She was the Shifter. But she hadn't sensed him until he spoke; and she should have been able to throw that knife so fast even a ward couldn't stop it. She had thought she was killing him when she threw it.

She hissed, hoping her cat's eyes glowed in the darkness. She couldn't attack him, not if she might lose. But he didn't have to know that. "That was a stupid thing to do, sorcerer."

"Why? Are you going to kill a man who protects your king?" Albin stroked the side of his beard. "I don't think Kaer would be happy with you if you did."

Isabel stood perfectly still. "That's assuming I believe you're protecting him."

The high sorcerer took another step out of the darkness, revealing the shimmering rainbow colors of the ward around him. "I think he's more suspicious of you than of me right now. Why else would he have asked me to keep track of your whereabouts, just in case you tried to leave?"

*That* rankled, more than she had expected. Because Kaer had assigned her a guardian? Or because she *would* leave, if only it were possible for her?

"Well," she snarled, "as you can see, I'm doing nothing of the sort. So why don't you pull one of your famous vanishing acts? I'm not in the mood for you right now."

"Shifters have moods?" The corners of Albin's lips

lifted in a snide smile. "Of course, it seems Shifters have a number of things the legends don't mention. Like divided loyalties."

Nothing he said should have bothered her, but she had been rubbed raw by memories. "I don't think you want to speak to me about divided loyalties, sorcerer. I am not the only one who served two princes."

"I serve no prince." Albin ran his fingers down the side of his robe. "I serve powers far greater, powers that will still exist years after this petty dynasty has vanished from the face of the world. Did you expect me to abandon my work, my records and experiments, just because a captain guard decided to overthrow a weak king? I don't care who sits on the Samornian throne, Shifter."

Isabel's laugh was oddly hollow in the vast, gloomy silence. "How noble. But you care who stands next to the throne, don't you? You didn't stay for your records and experiments. You stayed for your rich robes and the fine food and for people who watch you with awe and step out of your way when you walk." She took a step forward. "How wonderful it must have been for you when the Shifter was gone and there was no one to draw that awe away from you. How wonderful when the rogue sorceress died, and a raw young prince who would need your guidance ascended the throne. But then that prince went and found me, and I am more magical in my sleep than you are after a hundred spells. That's the real reason you agreed to help Kaer, is it not, sorcerer? Because Rokan had me."

Albin's lips twisted. "An odd claim to make, Shifter, when he never had you at all."

She stood for a moment with nothing to say, and he smirked at her, lips plump and smug between the dark bristles of his beard.

"You're going to die," Isabel said.

The expression on his face could not have altered more dramatically if she had shifted into a wolf right in front of him. "What?"

Isabel waited a full second, enjoying his fear. Then she said, "Eventually. You may be powerful, but you're mortal. How long can a sorcerer extend his life—a hundred years, two hundred?" She knew it wasn't even that long. "You *will* die, and your powers with you."

The high sorcerer raised his hand slightly, fingers curved. Isabel didn't think he was even aware of making the gesture, yet her whole body tensed. She was still afraid of this man. But he had no way of attacking her now, or he would have used it already.

"And you will live forever?" he spat out.

She lowered her eyelashes. "It does seem that way, doesn't it?"

Albin's fingers closed around empty air, and he looked at them in surprise before flicking his eyes back to her. Then he drew himself up, pulled his robe tightly around his body, and disappeared.

"Vanishing acts," Isabel muttered at the dust motes swirling in the space where he had been. But the scorn sounded hollow even to her. It was, after all, more than she could manage.

She stood, staring at the emptiness of the room, a stark reminder of what else she couldn't manage. She had made it here after the arrows flying past her had killed the king and queen, but not fast enough to save their children. The dynasty had ended right here.

Except it hadn't. She had a chance, now, to reverse that failure, to keep the right king on the throne. The king—just a boy, then—whom she should have restored to his throne a decade ago.

She wished she had. If she had remained with Kaer, she would never have fled back to her woods. She would have been at his side, guarding him. She wouldn't have returned to the castle a decade later to protect Rokan. She would have made sure Rokan died long ago.

And it would have been easy.

Why had she saved Kaer only to abandon him? What could possibly have kept her from his side?

She stood for a moment with the dank air moving in and out of her lungs. Then she turned and ran, through the cellars and up the narrow stone stairway. The silk of her gown wrapped around her legs as she ran; she reached down and ripped it off, flinging the heavy swath of blue silk down the stairs right before she slammed the door shut behind her. The silk fluttered soundlessly into the darkness; by the time it landed, she was already at the top of another staircase, in another hall.

Kaer was in his room—for the first time, she didn't think of it as Rokan's room—fast asleep. She smelled the rush of fear as he woke, and he was on his feet in a second with a knife in his hand.

"Shifter?" He didn't lower the knife. Moonlight spilled into the room from his open window. "What are you doing?"

She felt a pang, thinking of that dark-haired boy who had never again felt safe enough to sleep soundly. But she pushed that away. "I want to ask you a question. Put down the knife."

He didn't move. She did, and before he had time to react, the knife was in her hand and the blade was pressed against his throat.

She met his eyes for a full second before she stepped back, flipped the knife, and handed it to him hilt first. "If I wanted to kill you, you would be dead. But I want to protect you, so you're alive. Don't play games with me."

He took the knife without changing expression. Rokan could never have done that. "You *want* to protect me?"

"I was created to protect you. You have nothing to worry about."

His voice was perfectly cool. "Except why you're here interrupting my sleep."

She took two steps back, giving him enough space so he wouldn't feel threatened, and waited for him to sit on the bed. He didn't. He kept his grip ready on the knife, too; she could tell by the way the air currents eddied around his stiff, trembling fingers.

"How did I get you out?"

His face didn't so much as twitch. "I'm sorry?"

"The night your . . . the night of the coup. We were trapped in the laundry room, surrounded by soldiers. How did I get you out?"

"Spirits, Shifter! I was six years old and terrified. I don't remember anything about that day."

He was lying.

Isabel knew that as certainly as if he had blushed or avoided her gaze, though his eyes were rock steady. But if she hit him with the truth now, she would know. He was just off balance enough. She had several seconds, maybe less, before he would be as unreadable as stone.

"I didn't save you, did I?" she said.

Bull's-eye. He actually flinched.

"I left you behind." She said it with disbelief.

"You weren't yourself. You were half-mad." The words nearly tumbled over themselves. "And I was unconscious by then. I tried to climb up to one of the windows, and I fell and hit my head. You probably thought I was dead, that it was too late. You wouldn't have left if you knew I was alive. You're still my protector."

She was barely listening. He was right. She had been shifting, faster than thought, trying to think of how she could save them. There was no way she had simply left. No way she had failed . . . not without leaving behind so many dead soldiers she would have heard of the massacre, even a decade later.

"How did you live?" she asked.

"One of the soldiers, still loyal to my father. He smuggled me out. By the time I woke up, I was on the back of his horse."

"How did he do it?"

"Albin gave him a spell."

Isabel recoiled. *"Albin?"*

"He played both sides from the beginning. If you had managed to prevent the coup, he wanted insurance to keep you from killing him. The soldier wasn't supposed to use the spell if the coup succeeded." Kaer sneered. "Albin paid him well, and backed up his money with threats. It would never occur to a sorcerer that pure loyalty could count more than either of those."

"What happened to the soldier? Did Albin kill him?"

"No. The usurper did."

Isabel nodded, and Kaer walked to the window. Looking out at the darkness, he said savagely, "He killed everyone who could have protected me. My entire family. Anyone loyal." He drew in his breath. "And then, after training for years to kill him, I came to do it. And found you protecting his son."

He was going somewhere with this, but Isabel had lost him on the second sentence. "Your entire family?"

He turned around and stared at her. Isabel met his eyes, which were dark in the moonlight. "Your sister was older than you, wasn't she?"

Kaer put both hands behind him on the windowsill, bracing himself. "You think you saved her? Instead of me?"

"Have you seen her body?"

"The usurper said she was dead."

"He said you were dead, too." Isabel forced herself to stay still.

Kaer tilted his head back slightly, watching her. She could hear his fingernails scraping against the windowsill. "But she must be dead. You didn't stay with her. You went back to your woods without her."

He didn't want her to leave him and go running off to find his sister. Reasonable enough. And what he said was true. But still . . .

"How did I get her out?" Isabel wondered aloud.

Kaer shrugged. "If you did get her out, I wasn't conscious to see it."

Isabel pressed her palm against what was left of her skirt. "Your sister might be alive. Don't you care?"

"We'd probably be better off if she was dead," Kaer said. "And if she is alive, why isn't she here? She should be trying to take back what was stolen from us. Like I am."

"Maybe she's happy."

"More likely she's dead."

"I don't think Rokan thinks so."

Kaer went ash white. "What do you mean?" he whispered, though she could tell that he already knew.

Isabel dropped her hand. "You were wondering how he plans to legitimize his reign. This is how. He's going to find your sister and marry her."

"That's ridiculous!" Kaer snapped. The color flooded back into his face. "Find her where? Besides, my sister is as much a victim of his family's perfidy as I am. She'd stab him in his sleep."

He stepped forward, watching her with eyes that were hard, angry . . . and afraid. She ran her tongue over her upper lip. "You needn't worry, Kaer. You're here, and in danger. I'm not going off to search for her."

The split second before his nod told her that wasn't what he was afraid of. She turned and left before he could see, on her face, that she knew what it was he really feared.

She had saved the girl—back before her mind had been wounded, when she had been supremely confident in who she was and what she had to do. If it came down to it, she would side with the princess again, even against her brother.

She wondered if Rokan had thought of that.

# Chapter Seventeen

Isabel was not particularly surprised when, the next morning, she was woken before dawn by a summons from her king.

She arrived in the audience chamber to find it full of people. Kaer paced back and forth, bleary-eyed but immaculately dressed in dark green velvet. Clarisse sat on the couch with her feet tucked under her—a pose that declared, without defiance or ostentation, how unquestionably she felt she belonged there. Owain and Albin were both seated on one of the plush benches, and Daria stood rubbing her eyes near the fireplace.

*Daria?* Isabel thought, at first, that Kaer had made a stupid mistake. But in the few days since the coronation, she hadn't seen Kaer make a single stupid mistake, or a single ill-considered act.

She stepped into the room and closed the door behind her.

"We need to draw Rokan out," Kaer said without preamble, as soon as the door thudded shut. "I've had enough of waiting in this stone trap for him to make his move. We need to bring him here and end it. Now."

Owain raised a bushy eyebrow. "Can't it wait?"

"No, it can't," Kaer snapped. "I want him here before he has time to prepare. Before he can bring whatever"—*whomever*, Isabel thought—"he thinks can help him defeat me."

Owain and Albin exchanged the world-weary expressions of older men dealing with rash boys. They should know better, Isabel thought. But Kaer plainly didn't intend to share the truth Isabel had learned last night, and she wasn't about to do it for him.

"He'll know what you're trying to do," she said instead, and Kaer stopped pacing and turned to face her, a little less quickly than he might have. He nodded in agreement, the picture of confident command, but she could see the shadow of fear in his bloodshot eyes. He was afraid. Of her.

She rested her head back against the door. "How do you plan to get him here?" she asked. "Rokan won't come for a challenge, Kaer. He'll know there's a trap behind it."

Kaer went back to pacing. "We have to make him think

it's his decision, then," he said. "Make him think we don't know he's coming."

"Then why would he *be* coming?" Isabel asked—and as soon as the question was out of her mouth, she knew why Daria was there.

The girl stepped forward on cue. She was wearing a rose-colored gown and looked, Isabel had to admit, remarkably pretty. Her prettiness had been growing less and less understated since she had taken her place in Kaer's court. "He would come," she said, "for me."

*No, he wouldn't.* Did they think Rokan was stupid?

"He very well might," Clarisse agreed. She propped her elbow on the back of the couch and rested her head on her hand. "Spread a rumor that you're going to have her killed—maybe something about her secretly working on Rokan's behalf, he'll love that—and then have Albin loosen the wards around the castle for one night."

"Rather obvious, isn't it?" Albin said.

Clarisse slid her fingers through her hair. "Not really. The rogue sorceress told me once that no wards are constant; they're all subject to natural unpredictable fluctuations. Rokan will be waiting for one of those fluctuations. We'll just make sure it happens when we're ready for him."

Albin gave Clarisse a look of flat dislike. "Assuming he has magical assistance."

"It seems clear that he does." Clarisse turned away from Albin dismissively.

"And you really think he would come?" Kaer's voice forced Isabel's attention from the enjoyable sight of her two least-favorite people on the verge of attacking each other. The king had clasped his hands behind his back and paused at the end of the room. "That he would risk everything? Even if he's convinced Daria's secretly working for him, I find that hard to believe."

You would, Isabel thought. She braced both her hands against the door. "That's not relevant," she said. "He *won't* believe she's suddenly on his side. Rokan can be rash, but he's not stupid."

"You're right." The statement, startlingly, came from Daria. She moved closer to Kaer, brushing his taut arm with her fingers, and he took her hand almost absently in his. "But he'll still come. He would walk straight into a trap, knowing it might be a trap, if he thought I was in danger. I was the only person in the castle he loved."

"That isn't true." Isabel was surprised to hear herself speak, and at how cold her voice was.

"Really," Daria said, a brittle edge to her voice.

*I miss her.* As clearly as if she was still standing in his darkened room, she remembered the pain in Rokan's voice. What if Daria was right?

But Rokan had learned, since then, not to trust his feelings. Daria had started the lesson, and the Shifter had finished it. A bitter feeling rose in Isabel's throat, and she swallowed it hard.

"Yes," she snapped. "Really."

Daria stared at her with undisguised hate in her long-lashed eyes, but she said nothing.

"Isabel's the one who's been around him most," Kaer said. He disentangled his hand from Daria's and began pacing back across the room. "She would know. Not that I doubt your charms, Daria, but people have a way of falling out of love when you try to kill them."

"*I'm* the one who's been around him most," Clarisse snapped, sitting straight up on the couch. "And I think Daria's right."

Daria's head came up in surprise. Kaer crossed the room and took a seat next to Clarisse, who stiffened but didn't move, though Isabel could tell she wanted to. What she couldn't tell was whether Clarisse wanted to move closer to Kaer or farther away. "You do?"

"I do." Clarisse didn't turn her head toward him; she stared down at her hands, which were clenched on her knees. "I think Rokan knows about you and Daria—there are at least some people at court who are still loyal to him and could make sure information found its way to him. But he does still care about her." She glanced up at Isabel as she said it, her eyes hard as emeralds. "Once he hears the rumors about me and Kaer, he'll believe that Daria has been betrayed, and—"

"What rumors about you and Kaer?" Daria said.

Clarisse leaned back into the couch cushions, her eyes wide. Owain got to his feet and snapped, "You didn't tell her?"

Clarisse lifted her hand to her mouth in horror. Isabel didn't have to shift her sight to know there was a smile hidden behind her hand.

Perhaps because she was focused on Clarisse, she didn't sense any danger. The sound of swishing silk warned her, and she turned just as Daria flung herself at Kaer.

It wasn't a serious attack—Daria might have scratched up his face, but she didn't have the strength to hurt him. Nevertheless, Isabel reacted. She was across the room before Daria's fingers could touch Kaer, grabbing her by both wrists and flinging her to the floor.

Daria scrambled to her feet, sobbing, and went for Kaer again. Isabel grabbed one wrist this time, swinging Daria around to push her facefirst into the wall. She held her there with one hand, surprised by the vicious thrill that ran through her.

Spirits. She *hated* Daria.

"Let her go," Kaer said sharply, and Isabel obeyed,

more because of her own reaction than because of his. She stepped back, watching Daria crumple to the floor and dissolve in a storm of weeping.

Kaer knelt by Daria and put his arms around her shoulders, glaring over her head at Isabel. "What do you think you're doing?"

"She attacked you!" Isabel snapped.

"Do you honestly think I'm in danger from her? You're supposed to be helping me kill *him*, not attacking the few people who are truly on my side!"

"No one is on your side!" Isabel shouted at him. "No one but me!"

His face went flat and he turned back to Daria, pressing his lips to her hair. When he spoke, his voice was too low for anyone but Isabel to hear. "I wish I could believe that."

Isabel was shaking with rage and desperation. "Daria might love you, but she tried to hurt you anyhow, didn't she? Clarisse loved Rokan, but she'll help you kill him." As the words left her mouth, she suddenly realized how they *could* draw Rokan here; there was one person he would come for without question. And once she told Kaer how to lure Rokan to his death, she would erase this doubt forever. "I'm the only one who will stand by you no matter what, because *I* have no choice!"

"Try to sound a little happier about it, would you?" Clarisse murmured.

Isabel was across the room in a second, one hand on Clarisse's throat. Only the greatest effort of will kept that hand from squeezing tight.

Clarisse's neck muscles tensed beneath Isabel's fingers, but she didn't so much as flinch. "First Daria, then me? How fascinating that you feel a need to attack the exact two people who betrayed Rokan. Rather interesting choices for a creature who claims she has no choice."

"I *don't* have a choice," Isabel hissed. But even as she said it, a part of her mind protested. Clarisse was right. The attack on Daria had been unnecessary; the attack on Clarisse even more so. The Shifter, once she had figured out how to draw Rokan into the trap, should have told Kaer immediately instead of letting herself get distracted.

She had *wanted* to get distracted. Because she didn't want to tell him.

Isabel lifted her fingers from Clarisse's neck and stepped back. She turned to Kaer, opening her mouth to say what she should have no choice but to say. But she was arrested by the sight of the dark bruises on Clarisse's white throat. And on Daria's arm as well. Evidence of choices she couldn't have made.

270

Clarisse lifted an eyebrow at her. "Go ahead. It's not like you haven't betrayed him already."

"I'm not the only one," Isabel said despite herself. "And *you*—you're his sister—"

She stopped. The realization was so sudden, and so overwhelming, that for a moment the room faded away.

*Your sister might be alive*, she had told Kaer. Had said it straight to his face, had asserted that the Shifter would never have left without saving the princess. And had walked away from that conversation without realizing a thing.

In her mind's eye she saw the Shifter—as she had seen her in one of her dreams, from the outside, from terrified seven-year-old eyes. Shifting frantically from one form to the next. And then—

And then memory came to an end.

It must have been unendurable, for both of them. But it had been the only way to save her. For the Shifter, saving her was all that mattered. And that night the Shifter had seen only one way to save Kaer's sister. She had merged herself into the girl, giving the frightened young princess the power to shift into something else and escape from the death all around her.

Isabel wondered if she had screamed as the Shifter flowed into her, if she had tried to get away from the centuries-old power invading her mortal human body. She wondered if the Shifter had made a sound. If the Shifter had thought twice.

She no longer remembered how she had escaped the guards, but it could have been any one of a million ways. She could have become a mouse or a bird or a patch of fog. The Shifter had been strong in her then, had known what to do, had been able to guide the little girl to the Mistwood, where her magic could be replenished every second. No wonder her powers were so weak once she left it.

No wonder she had been so confused . . . filled with the Shifter's powers, the Shifter's needs, but with human emotions and human needs as well. She wasn't the Shifter, but she was. She wasn't human, but she was.

Isabel realized that she was shaking—actually shaking—and hastily shifted her muscles still. They were all watching her now, even Kaer, and she looked back at him with her face absolutely blank. The answer she had been about to tell him, had believed she *had* to tell him, trembled unspoken on her lips.

Maybe she should tell him the truth instead. Tell him she was his sister.

*We'd probably be better off if she was dead.*

I should hate him, she thought. But she didn't. She still remembered the brave young boy with dark hair and how much she had loved him. The Shifter didn't feel love, not even when she was giving her life; but the scared young princess had loved her brother, refused to go anywhere without him, cried with him when the soldiers came. He had told her not to worry and tried to protect her.

And now he needed someone to protect him. He wanted her to be the Shifter so badly. Even after she had hurt him by making mistakes the Shifter should never have made, protecting the wrong person, the son of the man who had come for him when he was a child. He had stepped in front of his sister back then, but deep down he had believed the Shifter would save them both. And the Shifter hadn't. She had chosen someone else.

It was the same dilemma. Rokan or Kaer. And she and Kaer had crouched together in a sealed room, years ago, while Rokan's father hunted them down.

Kaer was her brother. And he was the king. The king had to be protected.

She let herself follow that river of thought. Let herself believe in destiny and inevitability, that she was following a path forged by fate instead of making one on her own.

*How can you trust someone who would betray her own brother?* she had said.

Isabel closed her eyes and believed it. She spoke without letting herself think, because once she spoke it would be over. "He'll come for Clarisse."

"Clarisse?" Daria sneered, her voice still choked with tears. "He left her behind."

"He loves her. She's his sister." Isabel looked only at Kaer, who was still crouched near Daria. "He would come for her."

"Even though she betrayed him?" Owain said.

"At least she didn't try to kill him," Kaer pointed out, keeping his arms around Daria's shoulder but his eyes on Isabel's face. "Are you sure?"

Isabel closed her eyes briefly. There was no agonized decision-making left, no conflict. Just dull numbness. "Yes. I'm sure."

# Chapter Eighteen

TWO nights later Isabel found herself in Clarisse's room, waiting for Rokan to come so she could kill him.

She spent those two days in a daze, following instructions. She no longer made suggestions, or gave advice—she wasn't the Shifter, after all, just a human girl with a few odd powers.

I'm human, she thought every once in a while—not for any particular reason, just at random. *I'm human*. And she would stare down at her thin, pale hands that would never be anything else, never stretch into wings or curve into claws. She would feel her body, both more solid and more weak than it should have been, and know it was a trap. A trap she could never get out of, because it was a trap she had been born into.

She was trapped in her body and now in this room. The lamps had all been put out, and the delicate wood furniture and chests had been moved to the wall near the bed, leaving a large clear space for whatever was going to come. Clarisse's room was surprisingly large, once the clutter had been cleared away. There was nothing in the center of the room but a single plush chair, where Clarisse sat with her arms tied to the armrests and her legs bound to the chair legs. Isabel had tied the cords herself. Much to her disgust, Clarisse had agreed to their plan without a murmur.

Standing in the far corner of the room, she kept her eyes human, but her hearing was a cat's. She could hear Kaer in the corner to her right, his breathing fast and loud. The high sorcerer's breathing was slightly calmer, as were those of the two soldiers whom Kaer had decided could be trusted. But calmest of all was Clarisse.

She wondered how much longer she would be able to do this. If she returned to the Mistwood frequently, she might be able to keep her minor powers for a while, but she suspected that eventually they would drain away completely. She had been growing more human day by day. Eventually she would be all human, and the Shifter would be just a memory. And then not even that.

What would Kaer do with her, once she was no longer useful?

*We'd probably be better off if she was dead.* The phrase had been ringing in her head for two days. He had said it thinking she really was dead, of course; it didn't mean he meant it.

If he felt no loyalty for his sister, why should his sister feel loyalty for him?

The thought made her feel as if she had stepped off a high ledge. Then she realized there was someone else in the room.

He was breathing fast and deep, afraid but trying not to be. There was nothing else to indicate that he had arrived—no light, no sound, no sense of magic. It was a very good spell.

Nobody else knew he was there. She should tell them. She should grab him before he could move. Her hand touched the hilt of the dagger at her waist.

She concentrated and shifted her eyes.

He looked tired. His face was pale and drawn, his eyes underlined by dark shadows. His hair was neatly combed, though, and he was wearing black velvet. He stood tense and poised, peering around carefully, even though there was no way he could see anything in this darkness.

And still Isabel didn't move. She could see Clarisse, sitting in a chair in the center of the room, as still as Daria had sat when she was bait. Several paces behind the chair, Kaer stared straight ahead into the darkness. The high sorcerer's eyes were closed. One of the soldiers was fidgeting.

Rokan whispered, "Clarisse?"

Everything happened at once. Albin opened his eyes, and the room was full of light. Rokan squinted, momentarily blinded. The two soldiers drew their swords and stepped forward.

Clarisse turned in her chair and made a sharp, abrupt motion with her arm. The knife shot from her hand and imbedded itself into the chest of the soldier to her left. She was instantly on her feet with another knife. The second soldier dodged, and her knife sliced through a frayed tapestry before hitting the floor.

The rope Isabel had so carefully pulled around Clarisse's limbs lay slashed on the floor. Isabel didn't know where the knives had come from and had no time to figure it out. The first soldier was sprawled across the floor, blood spreading in a slow circle from underneath him. The second soldier whirled on Clarisse, who shouted, "I can take care of him! You take Albin!"

Rokan was already halfway across the room. The high sorcerer raised his hand. A flash of sizzling light hit Rokan in the chest and vanished. Rokan drew his sword and kept coming.

He aimed straight for the sorcerer's heart. Albin muttered something under his breath, and Rokan's blade vanished. Rokan grunted in shock, and—unable to stop his

momentum—stumbled into the high sorcerer's arms. Albin lifted him and threw him, harder than humanly possible, at the far wall.

Isabel didn't think. She sprang and collided with Rokan in midair, seconds before he would have hit the stone wall. They fell in a tangle, her briefly stone legs hitting the ground first, breaking their fall.

She heard Kaer yell something, and rolled to her feet. The true king, her brother, was running across the room at them, sword drawn. Isabel heard a hiss of power beside her as Rokan raised his hand. She leaned down and struck his wrist. A bolt of green fire missed Kaer by several yards.

Kaer flinched and slowed down. Rokan leaped to his feet, glaring. Not at Kaer. At her.

Isabel didn't need more than a glance to know that all her agonizing, all her thoughts and struggles about Kaer, had been wasted. This had never been about Kaer.

It was like the time in the woods when Rokan hadn't seen the knife coming. And she hadn't been thinking, in that split second, about what the Shifter would do or how the Shifter would feel. She had just acted.

Clarisse screamed. Rokan turned, away from both Isabel and Kaer, and Kaer leaped forward. Isabel shifted her hand to stone and grabbed Kaer's sword by the blade.

*"Shifter!"* Kaer shouted, as if to remind her of what she was. "I trusted you!"

No, you didn't, Isabel thought. But that was irrelevant. She pulled the sword out of his hand and looked at Clarisse. Clarisse was on the floor with blood all over her gown, but from the way she was screaming, it couldn't be fatal. The soldier sprawled next to her wasn't screaming at all.

Kaer followed her gaze. "Traitor," he snarled. "She'll get what you get."

Isabel remembered a much younger boy, with the same black hair and the same determined eyes, yelling at her. She had been older, but he had always taken the lead, and she had wanted his approval so desperately. She had followed him everywhere, and sometimes he had relented and they had laughed together and played tricks on their nurse. And he had always protected her. No matter how angry he was.

He didn't know who she was now, though. And suddenly she didn't want him to know. Let him think she had betrayed a prince, not a brother.

Rokan leaped to his feet, and there was a sword in his hand. It hadn't been there a second ago. Kaer lunged past her for his own sword, which she had thrown to the floor, but there was no way he could get to it in time. The air in the room was taut with power. Across the room, Albin sizzled with magic. For a moment Isabel saw his eyes glow.

She was shaking so hard it was distracting, but she didn't have the focus to shift her muscles steady, not when her weak human heart was being torn in half. Out of the corner of her eye, she saw Albin stretch out his hand.

And she killed her brother.

She killed him as surely as if it was she, and not Rokan, who plunged the sword into his chest. For one last blinding moment everything the Shifter had given her was hers again. She was across the room faster than humanly possible, faster than possible for any animal she knew of. For a split second she was the wind. And then she was solid again, and the hand that had slammed the dagger into Albin's throat was shaking.

And covered with blood. The blood was warm. Something unseen sizzled and crackled inches from Albin's palm but got no farther. There was nothing to stop Rokan's sword from sliding between Kaer's ribs.

Kaer screamed, in fury and pain but mostly fury, and fell to his knees. The high sorcerer didn't scream. He made a gurgling sound and started to turn his head toward her. He didn't finish the motion.

Isabel stepped back and let go of the dagger, watching him drop, glad he hadn't met her eyes. A globule of blood pooled between her thumb and finger and dropped all the way to the floor.

*Blood. On her hands, dripping to the floor as she ran out of the room.*

She made one last effort to remember, in detail, everything that had happened that day long ago. How she had tried to kill Rokan's father. How she had succeeded in killing someone else—anyone else. She was the Shifter; she must have killed people. She wouldn't have cared.

She tried to remember what it felt like not to care.

But she couldn't find the Shifter inside herself. She was nothing but a small, confused girl crouching on the floor and crying and holding her brother's hand.

"It was my throne," Kaer gasped. Blood bubbled from his lips with the words. "Mine, and you stole it from me."

"I'm sorry," Isabel whispered, even though he was talking to Rokan. She squeezed his hand tight, but he didn't look at her. "I'm so sorry."

Clarisse managed to raise her head and stare at her, eyes narrowed with pain and suspicion. But Rokan kept his eyes on the face of the man he had just killed.

"You would have destroyed it," he said.

Kaer opened his mouth, but this time only blood came out. His head fell back.

Rokan raised his eyes to Isabel then. For a moment she was afraid he would smile, or glare, or—worst of

all—thank her. Instead he said, "I'm sorry."

"He was my brother," Isabel said numbly, and didn't gauge anyone's reaction to that. Suddenly it didn't matter what they had known, what anyone had known, or how things should have happened. Nothing made sense. Kaer's hand was limp in hers, the bottom half of his face splattered with blood, obscuring the features that had always been so hauntingly familiar. As the Shifter, she was his. As a human, she was his, too, his blood, his family. It shouldn't have made a difference. Her actions should have been the same.

Except she was human, and she had a choice. So what she should have done, and what she did, were two different things entirely.

Rokan dropped the sword and went toward her, hesitantly, one hand out. His sleeve was soaked with blood. Isabel turned away and made one final, frantic effort to shift—into anything, anything at all. A wolf, a bird, a gust of air. She wanted to be mist, drifting through her forest, as cold and insubstantial as clouds.

Instead she was heavy and hot, and sobbing so hard her throat felt ready to burst. Rokan didn't try to touch her again. She heard him go and murmur to his sister and drape something over the bodies and say things about arrangements and coronations and the populace. She heard him say no sharply, and realized that Clarisse was suggesting they imprison her, the Shifter who was no longer trust-worthy, who never had been trustworthy. And Rokan was saying, "No. She stays."

And so she returned to the green-lined room she had woken up in lifetimes ago with no idea of who she was or what her destiny in this castle would be. Nor what it had been. She went to the window and remembered the last time she had stood here and thought about jumping. But then she had thought she would spread wings in midair and fly away. Now that she knew she couldn't fly away, she also knew she wouldn't jump.

*She stays.* For a searing moment she wondered if she had made the wrong choice, if she should have let the sorcerer work his magic. Because she *would* stay. If it had been Kaer who lived, she could have gone back to her forest and her mist and lived in a hundred different shapes for the rest of her life. But Rokan would be king, and she would stay with him. Her skin felt tight, holding her together, holding her in.

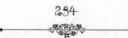

# PART IV

# ISABEL

# Chapter Nineteen

The Shifter would have been there. Helping Rokan put his kingdom back together, reassert his authority, maintain his legitimacy. Helping him deal with the currents and waves after the death of the true king, with the imprisonment of dozens of minor nobility, with the sudden appearance of the other true heir to the throne. The Shifter would not have let her own feelings keep her in her room, sleeping and sobbing and staring at the walls until everything had died down.

She spoke to Rokan only once, briefly, to explain what had happened to her and who she truly was. Rokan listened without visible disappointment, leaning against the wall of her room while she sat stiffly in one of the chairs near the bed. She kept her senses purely human, not wanting any inkling of what he really felt. Besides, purely human senses were all she had a right to.

When she was finished, Rokan pushed away from the wall and said, "I'm truly sorry, Isabel. Even if it meant you were able to save my life. I know being human was never what you wanted."

Damn what she had a right to. Isabel shifted her face expressionless, shifted away the moisture that welled up in her eyes, shifted away the burning in her throat. She sat still as a statue, hating the pity in those intent dark eyes.

When it became clear she wasn't going to reply, Rokan cleared his throat and said, "Owain disappeared. Nobody knows where he's gone."

Isabel drew in a breath and leaned against the back of the chair. "I'm not surprised," she said in the steadiest voice she could manage. "He's the sort to always plan for things going wrong, and then plan for that plan going wrong, too. I don't think he'll come back, though."

Rokan's eyes never left her face. "You were right, you know. You and Clarisse. I trusted Owain right up to the coronation. Clarisse couldn't make me listen, so she tried to find out his plans without telling me what she was doing. She didn't tell me she was going to stay behind to try to thwart them, either."

She didn't tell you a lot of things, Isabel thought.

"I thought he was an honorable man," Rokan added in a tone so bewildered she didn't have the heart to remind him that there was nothing dishonorable about deposing an imposter.

She said instead, very quietly, "And Daria?"

Rokan's eyes skittered away from hers, then back. "I sent her to live with one of the northern dukes. Duke Samar—he's a minor nobleman whose estate abuts Owain's. It's a poor land, and he has barely enough soldiers to hold it."

He also had a thirty-year-old son, recently widowed and reputed to be quite charming. Isabel didn't mention that.

Rokan smiled ruefully and ran a hand through his hair, leaving it sticking up in black tufts all over his head. "I suppose you think I should have executed her?"

"I don't think you could," Isabel said. "You love her."

Rokan studied her for a long time, but when he replied he focused on the wooden floor instead of on her face, his hands clenched at his sides. "I don't. I don't think I ever did."

Isabel couldn't look at him, either. She shrugged. "Maybe you don't anymore. That doesn't mean you never did."

"I was lonely. After my father died, I . . . all right, I loved her." His chest moved once with a quick, shallow breath, and he looked up, the pretense stripped from his face. "But Isabel, it was different from—I mean, it wasn't like—" He stopped, something like a plea in his eyes.

Isabel braced her hands on the chair cushion, refusing to meet his eyes. She had seen that plea once before,
right before she betrayed him; she couldn't bear to answer
it now, so soon after she had betrayed someone else. Not
when that betrayal was the reason she finally *could* answer
it. "What about the rest of the northern dukes?"

"They've mostly slunk quietly back to their estates." His
voice was dispassionate again, but his eyes matched neither
his words nor his tone. "Clarisse thinks we should do something public and messy to the ones I still have in custody, but
I don't see the point. There were too many people involved
in the conspiracy to punish them all. Clemency is a better
strategy in this case." He paused, then said carefully, "Do
you think I'm right?"

Human though she might be, she knew enough by now
of the intricacies of the northern alliances to be almost sure
he *was* right. She opened her mouth to answer, but then he
leaned forward eagerly, and suddenly *almost* was nowhere
near good enough.

"I can't—" The words came out bitter, burning her throat.
She gripped her knees. "I can't help you the way you want.
I'm not what I was. Not the Shifter. I'm sorry."

"I know what you are," Rokan said. "And it's *your* help
I want."

She shook her head and laughed, a short, harsh sound that

made Rokan flinch. "I'm nothing but a girl who once was the Shifter."

"A girl who once was the Shifter," he said, but his inflection gave the phrase an entirely new meaning, imbuing it with wonder instead of bitterness. "A girl who remained herself despite being the Shifter. Smart and funny and loyal and brave. There's nothing ordinary about you."

"You thought that was part of who I was. Now it's all I am. You need me to be the *Shifter*."

Rokan shook his head. His eyes were very intent on her. "That's not what I need."

She leaned back, laughing again. "You just haven't accepted the reality of what I am. That never was your greatest strength, was it?"

"That's not—"

"In the meantime," Isabel said, her voice emerging harsher than she had intended, "I just want to be alone. Please."

After a moment he nodded shortly and walked past her, his shoulders bowed. When he reached the door he hesitated, but he didn't turn his head. He walked away, and he didn't come back, though she spent the next half a day listening for his footsteps.

She had to emerge for the coronation. She stood next to the throne in a blue silk gown, no expression on her face,

and passed the crown to Rokan so he could put it on his head. The crowd erupted into cheers. She stared out at them, forcing a smile, and didn't even look at the new king. Her presence was proof that the last of the old royal family believed Rokan should be there.

Afterward she sat at Rokan's side during the banquet, staring at her plate, making monosyllabic replies to his hesitant, hopeful attempts to talk to her. As soon as she thought it wouldn't be noticeable, she went back to her room.

Clarisse was waiting there for her.

Rage flared up within her; this room was hers, her sanctuary, where nothing of her past or present or future was supposed to touch her. But the anger died before it got past her eyes. A part of her was still hundreds of years old, far too old to believe such foolishness. She closed the door behind her and said, "Why are you here? To tell me again that Rokan shouldn't trust me?"

"I'm here to find out why you're treating him this way," Clarisse said. She stood with her back to Isabel's bed, her elaborate ivory gown framed by the closed green canopies. "Can't you see how unhappy he is?"

"Am I supposed to believe you care?" The pins on her head were pulling her hair too tight, and had been for hours. Isabel started to shift the pain away, then changed her mind and began pulling out the pins instead.

Clarisse lifted one shoulder and let it drop. "He's my brother. Sometimes I do hate him, but he's still my brother. You don't understand that, do you?"

"Oh," Isabel said softly, "I think I do."

Clarisse was silent for a moment, shrewd green eyes assessing her. "Would you have killed him with your own hand in the end, if you had to?"

The smart thing would be to say yes. Kaer was already dead. But Isabel wasn't sure she could get away with it. The knowledge of what was happening to her seemed to have sped up the process; already, it took a great deal of effort to shift her voice. She shrugged. "I don't know."

Clarisse smiled faintly. "That's what Rokan said. I told him you would have."

Isabel dropped her hands to her sides. Her head no longer hurt, but there were curly tendrils of auburn hair tickling her face. "Do you want me to thank you?"

"No. I just want you not to tell Rokan that you weren't sure."

"Rokan is not an idiot," Isabel said.

Clarisse took a few steps forward—the better, Isabel thought, to judge her reaction. She concentrated on keeping her face still, though a part of her wasn't sure why she even cared. "Do you hate him for killing your brother? Is that what it is?"

"I don't hate him. He did what he had to do." Speaking the words aloud, Isabel suddenly knew they were true. She didn't hate Rokan; she could never hate him. It wasn't his fault that she had made her choice because of him. She spoke carefully, knowing Clarisse would repeat what she said to Rokan. "I just can't bear him being grateful to me for *letting* him."

Clarisse grimaced. "You think that's what he's feeling—grateful?"

"He should be. Everything worked out wonderfully for him, didn't it?"

"You really *don't* understand humans, do you?" Isabel looked at her blankly, and Clarisse sighed. "I suppose it did work out. Rokan doesn't have a Shifter anymore, but then he doesn't need as much protection. The rival prince is dead, the conspiracy broken. And with the one remaining member of the old royal family on his side, Rokan's rule is nearly secure."

There was a way to make it even more secure, but Isabel didn't say anything, just as she had said nothing when Rokan went over the political situation with her. It was too obvious to miss; Clarisse, and Rokan, would have thought of it already. It was odd, in fact, that both of them were studiously not mentioning it.

"He doesn't need the Shifter, does he?" Isabel said

sourly. "He has a knife-throwing sister to protect him."

For what was probably the last time, she caused surprise to flicker across Clarisse's face; but this time she hadn't intended to. Isabel straightened slowly, astonished at how stupid she had been. If she had spent more than one second this past week thinking instead of crying, she would have known.

"You can't throw knives," she said. "That was a spell."

Clarisse shrugged. "Spells are useful things. Why would I have wasted my time training with knives?"

Isabel remembered the dozens of times when she had sensed something, when Clarisse had appeared disoriented or unsteady, and Isabel had dismissed it as too much wine. Remembered the princess alone in her room, without a single maidservant or lady-in-waiting to see what she was doing. "Rokan got his spells from you."

"Of course. Did you think my father actually trusted Albin? He had a rogue sorceress begin training me when I was ten years old."

"I'm surprised he trusted you," Isabel said.

"He didn't. But my father understood emotions, even though he didn't have any. He let me take care of Rokan and made sure we faced an array of common enemies . . . nasty governesses, sadistic guards. Rokan was so small and helpless." For a second Clarisse's mask slipped and there was something real on her face. "My little brother. I used the magic I learned to protect him."

And then the Shifter had come, and Rokan hadn't needed her protection anymore. Isabel understood, suddenly, the light in Clarisse's eyes at the coronation, when the Shifter had stood back and let Rokan be taken.

She wasn't the Shifter anymore, but Clarisse was still watching her with that banked hatred in her eyes. Still afraid that Rokan would put her first? Isabel skittered around that thought, focusing instead on the implications of Clarisse's revelation.

"So it all came from you," she said slowly. "The translocation spells. Rokan's sword at the coronation. The poison that disappeared from the goblet. The knives—"

And the one other piece of untraceable magic.

Isabel almost stopped breathing. She saw by the expression on Clarisse's face that the princess knew she had figured it out.

"You," she said, too stunned to be angry. "You killed Ven."

Clarisse started to step backward, but stopped in midmotion and lifted her chin. "Who did you think it was? Rokan never realized how dangerous you could be. I did, from the start, but of course no one would listen to me. That stupid boy told you the truth about the bracelet, and he was about to tell you the truth about Kaer. He would have turned you against us."

"I already knew about Kaer." Isabel shook her head, remembering how she had forced Ven to answer her. "You killed him for nothing."

"I didn't know that. But I knew what you were capable of. I had to protect him."

"Protect *yourself*."

Clarisse pulled her shoulders back, ready to attack—an attack that, for the first time since Isabel's arrival, would not be completely ridiculous. Clarisse could use her magic openly now, and Isabel was—almost—just a powerless girl. Isabel moved into a fighting stance and hoped Clarisse didn't realize that.

But Clarisse merely smiled, leaving Isabel to wonder whether she had been planning to attack at all. Her smile was sharp and hard-edged, and her voice was almost calm. "What difference does it make?"

"It *will* make a difference." The sound of her own voice—low, steely, icy—was alien to Isabel. "I'm part of the court now. I'll be here for a long, long time. I know what you did, and I am very patient." She stepped forward, and Clarisse stepped back. But still the princess's expression didn't change. "If you're smart, Clarisse, you'll leave now, and make sure I never hear from you again."

Clarisse smiled, a real smile, and tossed her hair back. "But I've never been that kind of smart, Isabel." She broke their locked gazes and raised one eyebrow. "And I'm not very good at staying out of trouble."

"Have it your way."

"I usually do."

"Back when we first met," Isabel said, "you said that you always do."

Clarisse walked past her, opened the door, and stepped into the hall. Isabel watched her go, and stood for a long time staring at the empty doorway before she shut the door again.

Rokan came to her room early the next morning. Isabel, who still made the effort to listen for his approach, was sitting up in bed wearing the green and white riding outfit he had given her the first time he saw her.

He took a small step into her room, then another; he stopped and opened his mouth. His eyes locked on hers, half-afraid but determined. Like her riding outfit, his expression reminded her of the day they had met, when he had ridden into the Mistwood to summon a magical creature who might be his death.

He crossed the room in a few sudden, decisive strides and pulled himself up on the foot of the bed, a few feet

away from her. He set his chin and said, "You were wrong."

She kept her back straight, meeting his eyes but keeping her expression veiled. "Wrong about what?"

"I don't want you to be the Shifter." Rokan's voice was quiet, and her human sense of smell told her nothing about how he felt. "I haven't wanted that for a long time. Since before I knew it was possible for you to not be the Shifter." A pause, and then—so quietly that even she could barely hear him—"Since before I knew I loved you."

Without warning—though the Shifter would have seen it coming—he leaned forward and took both her hands in his.

The contact went through her with a shock. She hadn't felt his hand around hers since that day in the Mistwood; she had forgotten the firm, callused warmth of his fingers. For a moment she almost gave in to the urge to rest her cheek against his tunic and feel his arms around her. She had wanted to do just that for so long. He was perfectly still, hardly breathing, waiting for her.

She drew in a deep shuddering breath and pulled her arms back. Rokan dropped her hands as if she had shifted them to fire. She averted her eyes, not quite quickly enough to avoid seeing the hurt in his, and struggled to find her voice.

Before she could, Rokan said—in that same quiet voice— "Is it because I killed him?"

"No," she whispered. "You had no choice."

"I wish I could have done it differently." He clenched the blanket, holding his hands there with an effort. "I wish it could have happened in a way that didn't hurt you. I wish that more than anything."

Isabel lifted her eyes to his face and made her voice gentle. "I need a horse."

He went absolutely still. "What?"

"I have to go to the Mistwood."

"Isabel—" He stopped, closed his eyes. He unclenched his fingers one by one, pressing them down, before he opened his eyes. They were dark as night and watched her with a hopeless intensity. "Of course. If that's what you need to do."

His face was so bleak her heart twisted, and she couldn't help herself. She slid closer to him and placed her hand gently against his cheek. She could feel the faint stubble that meant he hadn't been shaved yet that morning, the taut line of his jaw. He lifted his hand to hold her fingers there, then let it drop back to his knee and held her instead with his eyes.

"Come back," he whispered.

Isabel couldn't speak. She nodded her head slowly, once, never moving her eyes from his.

He smiled then, the smile she loved—wide and

unrestrained, alive with joy, as if he were free. And this time she finally did what she had been too cautious to do before, what she had wanted to do since that first day in the Mistwood.

She ran her hand down his arm, twined her fingers with his, and smiled back.

The next morning Isabel rode to the Mistwood.

The trees seemed less hostile this time when she rode into them. They still weren't welcoming—not as they would have been for the real Shifter—but now she knew why. She rode to the center of the woods, dismounted, and carefully hobbled her horse. She knew she wouldn't be returning as a wolf.

She waited for hours, sitting cross-legged in a bed of ferns, soaking up the power that had, she strongly suspected, given birth to the Shifter in the first place. Then she shifted.

It was hard. Not impossible, as it had been in the castle, but harder than the last time she had been in these woods. She shifted into a cat—because she had lied to Clarisse back in the beginning; it *was* her favorite form—and stretched luxuriously, arching her back and digging her claws into a pile of dead leaves.

She became a wolf, and then a bird. One last time she soared above the treetops, stretching her wings to catch the wind sweeping in from the south. She circled back and dove,

landing on a low tree branch. She had planned to be a bird last, but on impulse she shifted into a squirrel and ran down the trunk. And then, finally, she became human again.

The mist swirled around her briefly and dissipated. Isabel stood for a second watching it, wondering what happened to each bit of the Shifter that had been slowly seeping out of her for weeks. Did it dissolve back into wind and fog, conscious-less and purposeless, nothing more than a breath of air? Or here, in the woods where the Shifter had been born, was it coalescing slowly, reforming, shifting back into what it had once been—or into something altogether different?

The Shifter wouldn't have wasted time wondering about it. Isabel lifted her chin, felt the breeze caress her face, and smiled.

Then she mounted and nudged her horse lightly with her heel. The horse was all too happy to get out of the woods and broke into a full gallop as soon as he was able to. Isabel let him. Her hair, red-brown and tangled, whipped out behind her as she leaned low over his neck. When they had passed far enough beyond the last tree, she reined him in and looked back. The mist wreathed among the trees. It was probably only her imagination that made it look stronger, more alive, than it ever had before.

Her horse nickered and pulled at the reins. Isabel let him have his head, and they set off for the castle at a gallop.

# Acknowledgments:

A million thanks to . . .

My amazing editor, Martha Mihalick, both for loving that first manuscript and for seeing how it could be even better;

All the incredible people at Greenwillow, especially Virginia Duncan and Lois Adams, for helping to make it better;

The HarperCollins marketing group, especially Patty Rosati, Emilie Ziemer, and Laura Lutz, whose enthusiasm for *Mistwood* is so exciting;

Paul Zakris, for a jacket that makes me smile every time I see it;

My agent, Bill Contardi, for his experienced and reassuring advice;

My father, for introducing me to fantasy in the first place, and my mother, for not making him throw out all his old science fiction books;

Tzipporah and Shmuli, for providing my first experiences of conflict and high intrigue;

Tova, always my first editor;

Miriam, my web-tech and cheerleader;

Raymond and Sandra Cypess, for consistent support and encouragement;

Michael A. Burstein, for advice along the way;

Shanna T. Giora-Gorfajn, for editing and playground support;

And last but not least, to my husband Aaron, who married me just a month after I left law to try this full-time writing thing. Thank you for supporting my decision, for never acting like it wasn't important, and for encouraging me to become a non-reclusive writer. This would never have happened without you.